The Smithsonian Connection

THE SMITHSONIAN CONNECTION

Daryl Lucas

Tyndale House Publishers, Inc.
Wheaton, Illinois

Books in the Choice Adventures series

Cover Illustration copyright © 1991 by John Walker
Library of Congress Catalog Card Number 90-72060
ISBN 0-8423-5026-8
Copyright © 1991 by The Livingstone Corporation
Printed in the United States of America
99 98 97 96 95 94 93 92 91
9 8 7 6 5 4 3 2 1

"**S**o what do you want to do, Willy?" asked Pete.

"I don't know. What do you want to do?"

Pete let out a sigh and looked down at the melting ice cream giving way to the spoon he was eating with. "I don't know."

Sam and Chris just shrugged their shoulders. "Never knew summer vacation could be such a drag," said Chris.

It was a hot, humid July Thursday in the Washington, D.C., suburb of Millersburg; "ninety-five degrees with 90 percent humidity" was the forecast. This kind of hot makes it feel like the air is sweating on *you* instead of the other way around, so they had all just gotten ice cream sundaes of various concoctions at the Freeze, a cozy ice cream shop and favorite meeting place of the "Ringers." But it was only ten o'clock in the morning, and a whole lot of this summer vacation day was left to kill. They were bored.

What's worse, Jill and Tina, the two girl members of the gang, were both at summer camp. As much as the guys didn't want to admit it—which, make no mistake, they didn't—they missed having them around.

Pete sat up and pretended to have come up with a brilliant idea. "I know, Chris," he said. "Let's do whatever *you* want to do!"

Chris was ready. "I'm all for doing what *Sam* wants to do."

6

Sam hardly blinked. "I think we should do whatever *Pete* wants to do."

A female voice chimed in from across the room. "I'm glad you guys aren't running the country." It was Betty Metz, speaking from behind the counter as she wiped it down. She owned and operated the Freeze and was a good friend to the Ringers.

"OK, Betty, what do you think we should do?" asked Chris.

"Got all day?"

They nodded.

"Got any money?"

"A little."

"Why not go down to the Air and Space Museum?" It was the kind of suggestion most people would jump on. The National Air and Space Museum was one of the many famous Smithsonian Institution museums in Washington, D.C., and it was also one of the most popular—and for good reason. It had all the good exhibits—jets, rockets, actual capsules that flew to the moon, the original Wright Brothers plane, Skylab, moon rocks, a wind tunnel, and just about everything that ever had anything to do with flight. Practically *everybody* who ever visited thought it was awesome and wanted to come back, with the possible exception of the one or two who had been there a hundred times and had gotten sick of it.

Sam had been there a hundred times. When he heard Betty's suggestion, he shielded his eyes in agony and yelped, "No! Ugh! Not the Air and Space Museum!"

"*Ugh?*" said Willy, spreading his arms in disbelief.

"That's a *great* idea! The Air and Space Museum is *awesome!* Pete, you would love it."

Pete was into electronic gadgets, and the Air and Space Museum certainly had its share of those. In fact, he was building a model of the space shuttle at home, one that you put hobby rockets in and can launch with a remote control. The shuttle's booster and external tank would separate from the shuttle just like the real thing, then parachute down to the ground, followed by the shuttle itself. You had to be careful not to launch it around buildings or trees, or else you'd lose it for sure.

"That's a rotten idea, guys," argued Sam. "My parents used to clean that place, so I've been in it a hundred times. It's pretty neat, but I'm tired of it."

"Yeah, but they get new stuff all the time, you know," Pete continued. "The last time I saw it was, like, second grade or something. I'll bet they have a big model of the space shuttle and a whole bunch of new flying gadgets and electronic junk in there."

"Have you got a better idea, Sam?" asked Chris. He was good at letting everyone else air their opinion, then trying to get everyone to agree. He liked his friends, and he liked it when they were all getting along.

"How about . . . ," Sam paused, wrapping his lips around a huge spoonful of Oreo ice cream. "Hmph bcht blupdt gurngle wyan."

"How about you talk without a gallon of ice cream between your teeth," said Chris. "Miss Whitehead would have given you one of her looks and said something like, 'Young man, if it's worth saying, it's worth saying with an

8

empty mouth!'" Ever since the Whitehead family had
moved back to town, the name came up often.

Sam swallowed. "I was buying time, Kimosabe." He
looked away and took another spoonful. The rest of them
just waited. The mention of Miss Whitehead subdued the
conversation a little. She had been Chris and Willy's
Sunday school teacher until two years ago, when she died
unexpectedly. The two boys missed her, and the others
knew it. She had been their friend as well as their teacher.
When she taught, they wanted to learn. Silence persisted
for a few uncomfortable moments.

Sam thought as fast as he could. Finally, with a gleam
in his eyes, he pointed his spoon at the others and shook it
as he said, "I know. How about we go to the bridal registry
at Penny's. We could all register as brides!"

Willy opened his mouth wide and laughed, causing a
mouthful of butter pecan to dribble down his chin. Chris
and Pete just looked at each other and slapped their
foreheads.

"Look, Sam," said Pete, "we don't have to read all the
signs. We can just go through and look at gizmos. Think of
it: the space shuttle, rockets, stuff like that. If we get really
bored, we can go to some other buildings. They've got
history, art, natural junk, all kinds of buildings."

"Hey!" sparked Willy suddenly, "I'll bet you know
about some secret passages or stuff we don't know about,
since your parents used to work there. You could give us
an 'unauthorized tour' of the place!"

This idea got everyone pretty excited. What could be
more interesting than a hunt for secret passages? They had

found some in the church, hadn't they? Why not in a museum? And surely someone whose parents worked there would know a lot about it. Sam had visited there lots of times over summer vacations because he could get free meals in the cafeteria.

Sam felt flattered to be the one with "inside information." He didn't really know about any secret passages—unless a few broom closets count as secret passages—but the others sure thought so. And the fact that they seemed sure of it made him feel quite important.

CHOICE

If Sam admits that he doesn't know about any secret passages, turn to page 16.

If Sam pretends that he does, turn to page 29.

10

Pete decided to play it safe and explain things to the guys before doing anything stupid. Once they were in the theater, they took seats front and center. Pete made sure he sat in the middle and wasted no time getting their attention.

"Guys, guys, this is weird. This is really weird," said Pete out of breath.

The gang leaned toward him from both directions. "What? What?" said several of the others trying to calm him down.

"While Sam was talking about the museum, this guy was talking to the woman—you know, the one who told us we should get in line early and all that? Well, I heard him say my dad's name, or at least I thought I did, so I turned around and asked him about it—if he knew my dad, you know, from church or something. And he looked weird in the first place—you know, real serious, like a hit man. And when I say—when I ask him if he knows my dad, his eyes bug out like he saw a mongoose. 'I beg your pardon?' he says, like an English guy without the accent, real careful and polite, but like he's trying not to act surprised when he really is, you know? And he was mad. So I said, 'Maybe you know him from church—Kyle Anderson, taller than me but has less hair?' and he just keeps staring at me, with his eyes bugging out . . ."

"Well, you do look a little like a mongoose," mumbled Sam.

"Shhh, be quiet!" Willy flicked him.

"And then," finished Pete, "he like gets real mad and says, 'No, I don't believe so.' Then he just says, 'Excuse me,' and takes off real fast." Pete told it almost exactly as it happened. He was very precise about everything. Sometimes this annoyed the guys because it made him take a long time to do things. But for things like this, when they wanted to hear every detail, it came in handy.

"The guy did look pretty weird," said Jim.

"Have you seen him before?" asked Chris.

"No, I don't *think* so," answered Pete. "He looks familiar, but I can't remember if I've seen him before or not. Either way, if he knows my dad, why did he act so, so—"

"Shocked to see you," finished Jim.

"Right," confirmed Pete.

"And why did he lie about knowing your dad," added Chris.

"Yeah."

"Are you sure he said your dad's name?" asked Jim.

"Yeah, positive."

Slight pause.

"Well, the world is full of kooks," observed Sam, not ready to believe there was anything to Pete's story. "He's probably just an escapee from St. Elizabeth's."

"But there may be something to it," Pete insisted.

"How do you know?" asked Sam.

Pete whispered, "You guys know my dad's an FBI agent, but I don't think I've ever told you he investigates technology theft." Silence.

"Vanilla dynamite, that's right!" mused Sam.

Just then the lights started to dim, and several people shushed the guys. They were dying. They couldn't get up and leave—they were down front right in the middle. They were trapped. They had the best seats in the house, and they didn't even want them.

Suddenly Chris remembered the woman—what had become of her? She hadn't walked away had she? Chris was sitting two seats over from Pete, so he leaned over and whispered, "What about the woman?"

Pete thought for a second, then whispered back, "I don't know. I didn't notice."

"Did she come in with us?"

"I don't know."

Suddenly Chris felt a strong hand squeeze his shoulder. "You jerks better shut up, or I'm going to ruin your visit," said a deep voice directly behind him. There was no more talking during the movie.

The bright sunshine streaming through the huge glass sections in front of the museum hurt their eyes as they came out of the theater. It reminded them that they had been thirsty ever since they'd arrived but hadn't even so much as visited a water fountain. By now they were having visions of large, ice-infested oceans of dark pop.

They headed over to the cafeteria.

CHOICE

Turn to page 46.

It was now 5:50, and Zeke was starting to get mad. He knew, for sure, at least three things: (1) the guys knew where to meet him but didn't show; (2) they weren't in the museum because it was closed; and (3) they had to be outside the museum somewhere.

But where? They could be waiting outside the south entrance, after getting confused about where to meet him. Or they could be hiding in the bushes, waiting to see him panic.

He strolled over to the hot dog vendor and bought a hot dog and large Coke, then began circling around the building, checking the street vendors for signs of the gang as he headed for the south entrance. The south entrance was locked up just like the north, with no sign of the gang. He was going to pound them good.

Once they had decided to wait until nine o'clock, they all relaxed (except Willy) and sat down, Pete and Jim on the boxes and the others on the floor. After going full throttle all day, and especially the last few minutes, they were exhausted. The heat in the closet made them feel it even more.

Willy and Sam hadn't forgotten their feud, either. Silence hung over the gang like a dark cloud. Willy let out a huge, frustrated sigh and stared at his feet. Most of the time, he and Sam got along great. But not always.

Chris hated it when that happened. "Well, since there's nothing to do but wait, we might as well relax."

"Easy for you to say," said Willy.

"Willy," said Pete, "we're going to get out of here. Don't worry about it."

"I think I'll worry about it anyway, OK?" Willy snapped back. Sam held his tongue.

Jim made a sound like he wanted to say something. Everybody looked at him. They could tell he was thinking something they wanted to know as he shrugged his shoulders and said, "I think it's pretty neat that Sam confessed. I don't know if I would have done it."

Doink. Friends love at all times. Several long seconds went by as everyone digested Jim's comment.

Chris nodded his head. "It did take a lot of guts."

Suddenly Willy realized Jim was right. Sam had gone out on a limb when he told them he lied. He trusted them. In fact, they were in that closet because what he confessed was private and embarrassing, and he wanted only his best of friends—the only ones in the world he could really trust—to hear it.

Willy found himself feeling like he'd let Sam down, so he looked over at his quick-witted friend and smiled. "Most of the time it's just easier to let it go," he said. "Nobody catches you. You just let everyone think you're cool." He wiped at his face and nodded at Jim. "You're right, Jim. And I'm sorry I blew up at you, Sam. It wasn't your fault. You didn't know they were going to lock the door."

Sam accepted the apology and smiled back. "I'm sorry I got us locked in here."

This must be what the Bible means by "love covers a multitude of sins," thought Jim.

"As long as none of us has to go to the bathroom, what's the difference?" said Willy. "It'll be an adventure."

The gang chuckled. They hadn't thought of that.

Pete yawned. "Actually, staying awake could be the main adventure for me. What time is it?"

Chris looked at his watch and said, "Six o'clock. Do you want to take a nap?"

CHOICE

If they take a nap, turn to page 123.

If they don't take a nap, turn to page 93.

16

Sam found himself swept up in everyone's excitement. Before he could even think, he stammered, "Y-yeah, I guess I do know some places that are, like, hidden—"

"Yes!" exclaimed Willy. "I knew it!"

"I-I-I wouldn't really call them *secret,* though," Sam continued. "*Secret*—that's a pretty strong word. Willy, just what do you mean by *secret?* Because what most people call *secret*—that wouldn't really apply to broom closets, do you think? I mean, they are, like, hidden. But *secret* secret—that's like, more heavy."

"Heavier," Betty corrected.

Willy calmed down.

"Well, who needs secret passages?" said Pete. "We already got some in the church. Besides, this is the twentieth century. What museum would have secret passages?"

"But who says there *aren't?*" said Willy. He wasn't ready to give up the idea of hidden passages. "I mean, they're secret, right? Maybe we'll stumble upon some like we did in the old church."

"The main thing," said Chris, trying to steer their attention from the secret passages, "is that we'd be having a great time together."

"Yeah," agreed Pete and Willy.

"Even if you didn't give us an *un*authorized tour,"

Willy continued, "you could still give us a real tour. Or, I know, Sam," he said, getting excited again, "you could tell us which exhibits to *avoid*. It would save us from waiting in line for all the dullsville stuff." The others agreed.

"And," Pete said leaning forward, as if sure that what he was about to say would be the clincher, "it's *air-conditioned*."

"We could get Jim's granddad to take us to the Metro station," Willy concluded. "Jim could come along too! How about it, Sam? With Jill and Tina at camp, you gotta come!"

Sam thought for a second. On the one hand, he hated the museum. On the other, he wanted to be with his friends.

CHOICE ➡

If Sam decides to go, turn to page 84.

If he decides not to go, turn to page 59.

18

Pete nervously shook Scorpion's hand.

"I'm sorry about that unfortunate exchange back in front of the theater," said Scorpion politely. "It's just that you caught me off guard. I had just gotten a call from a man named Kyle Andersen. The topic of our conversation was rather private, so I was, shall we say, knocked off balance when you claimed to be his own son." He chuckled. "A bit angry at the coincidence, you might even say."

I'll say, thought Pete.

"In any case, I hope I didn't spoil the movie for you," he continued. "It's quite good, don't you think?"

They nodded their heads, but no one said anything.

"Well, I am extremely busy, so I must be running along. . . ."

Just then Willy blurted out, "What do you do?"

Scorpion was again caught off guard but covered it well this time. "Martin Bluewater, Donations and Acquisitions. Glad I ran into you, uh . . ."

"Pete," said Pete nervously.

"Pete." He smiled. "Bye-bye, and enjoy the Air and Space Museum!" He turned on his heels and walked briskly away.

Chris turned his back to Scorpion and faced the gang and whistled. "Do you belieeeeeve . . ."

"So that's Bluewater," mumbled Sam, remembering the times he'd seen his office.

"I don't trust this guy," said Pete.

"Why?" asked Willy, a little surprised.

"You know," recalled Pete, "how the Bible talks about how Satan is an angel of light? How sometimes he makes sin look pretty so people will like it, but when you look closer it's ugly and slimy? That's kind of how I feel about this guy."

"Ugly and slimy?" asked Sam.

"It just seems to me like he's hiding something."

The gang paused in thought. Pete was a bit of a social misfit. He liked school; he could get sidetracked reading the signs at museums; he could even forget to go to the bathroom. But that was because he noticed things. Subtle things. Things most people miss. The guys had learned to respect that.

"But how do we know he's telling the truth?" asked Pete. "He even admitted he lied just now."

"Well," said Willy, "he *seems* nice enough. And he sure wasn't afraid of being seen in public by all of us. He even told us his name and that he works here. Doesn't seem to me like he has much to hide."

"There is a Martin Bluewater who works here," said Sam. "I've seen his office. Besides," he added, "what's he gonna do in the middle of the Air and Space Museum? There must be a thousand people here."

"Yeah, but I can understand why Pete's nervous," said Chris. "The guy could be lying, you know. Maybe we should call Pete's dad and tell him what happened."

Pete thought that was a good idea, but he could tell Sam and Willy were anxious to get on with the day. He decided to give Jim the deciding vote. "We'll do whatever you think we should do, Jim."

CHOICE

If they call, turn to page 149.

If they don't call, turn to page 55.

They went to the security desk and paged both Pete and Zeke. "Clarence Washington and Pete Andersen," the announcer said slowly, "please meet the Ringer party at the security desk."

"Hey, that's the first time we've gone public!" said Sam.

Zeke didn't take long in getting there. They kind of hoped Pete would show up too, but of course he didn't. It was 3:10.

Zeke nearly lost his contacts when he heard the Ringers explain their kidnapping theory. "You guys—," he said, holding his side with laughter, "you guys are too much! Kidnapping—oh, my side! Oh, my goodness. Oh—"

"Older brothers," Willy mumbled.

The breathless Zeke somehow managed to continue. "Kidnapping." He shook his head. "Oh, I don't think so. Lost? *Maybe.* Kidnapped—I don't think so!" he gasped.

"Well," Sam defended, a little upset, with volume, "have you got a better explanation, Oh Great Zucchini?"

"Yes, I do," he said, calming down a little. "One, he could have gotten sidetracked. Two, he could have gotten lost. Three, he could have run into that donations guy—"

"Scorp himself?" asked Willy, his eyes bugging out.

"Yeah—and gotten a VIP tour of the place."

No way.

"I mean, why not?" Zeke continued. "Pete's a hacker, isn't he?"

"He is not a hacker," protested Chris. "Hackers do illegal stuff. Pete's just smart. He doesn't do illegal stuff."

"OK, OK. The point is he's a computer whiz, right?" They nodded. "And—what did you call him—Scorpion?" he chuckled, "is some employee of this place—could be that they bumped into each other again, and he invited Pete up to his office to see all the neat stuff that was getting donated."

The problem with this was that it made a little sense. Few things are worse than admitting your older brother could be right. It's like surrendering. There's no honor in it.

Finally, Willy managed, "Well, how come he didn't meet us back at Skylab and tell us that? He should have met us back at Skylab. And why didn't he answer our message over the loudspeakers?"

Zeke looked thoughtful. "That's a good point," he said after a brief pause.

Phew. Some honor salvaged.

Zeke was trying hard not to laugh, but every time he heard the word *kidnapping* in his mind he could hardly hold back a major guffaw. He did his best to think about helping the guys instead of thinking about kidnapping. He took a deep breath. "OK. It's now been—what . . ."

"Forty minutes," said Sam.

". . . forty minutes since you got separated, and Pete still hasn't returned. You guys waited . . ."

"About a half hour."

". . . about a half hour." Zeke thought for a moment,

then nodded his head. "That should have been plenty of time."

Exactly, thought the guys. The gang was learning what it feels like not to know what has happened to someone you care about. It's fine for someone else to think about it logically and come up with good reasons why the person's missing, but that sick feeling in your stomach just won't go away until you see that person again.

"Did you check the Gemini capsule?" asked Zeke. "That's where we agreed to meet if we got separated."

The whole gang shook their heads. "He would have had to go right past us at Skylab to get there," said Sam.

"Oh," said Zeke. There was another uncomfortable pause.

"How come he didn't come back?" Willy repeated. "He wouldn't just go off by himself without telling us."

Zeke looked at his brother with genuine concern. "Look guys," he said, "if Pete is missing, he'll meet us at the Gemini exhibit eventually. I'll wait there for him while you guys check out the museum. If he doesn't show by a certain time, we'll call home and see what they say."

"Can we call the FBI first?" asked Sam. "I mean, if he really is in trouble, and his dad knows about what's going on, shouldn't we call them as soon as we can?"

CHOICE ➡

If they call the FBI first, turn to page 138.

If they search for Pete first, turn to page 79.

Pete slowly moved closer to the two so he could hear them speaking. He had to strain to hear.

". . . fault-tolerant encryptor? It's been sent to the museum—we got it today."

The woman in glasses said something in reply, and then, "Smithsonian Connection?"

"Yes," the taller man said disgustedly.

". . . on duty tonight?"

The man nodded. The woman sighed and looked worried and barely uttered her next words, which Pete couldn't hear. And then, something about "Victor."

The man answered with a look, which Pete couldn't see since his back was turned. Pete was getting frustrated. Finally the man said, "He'll know what it is as soon as he sees it. Now it's just wait and see." Pete could hear the man better than the woman, so he moved closer as she spoke.

She sighed and mumbled, ". . . Ph.D. . . . fault-tolerance . . . going to be—"

"Pete! Come on!" Chris shoved him gently from behind, causing him to bump into the woman. The embarrassed Pete apologized and wheeled around to see the line moving quickly.

As he rejoined the gang, the woman said to the other, "Tell Kyle thanks!"

"Will do!" the man replied.

Inside the theater, Pete daydreamed. His dad. Fault-tolerance. Smithsonian Connection. Encryptor. The two must have assumed he wouldn't know what those big words meant.

Willy waved a hand in his face. "Hello-ooo, is anybody home?" The gang had no idea what Pete had been thinking, but he was obviously acting strange.

Pete blinked and smiled, embarrassed. "Just daydreaming."

"Did you even hear the question?" teased Sam.

Pete chuckled and said, "Uh-uh."

"Maybe he'd rather be reading signs," teased Willy.

"What do you want to see next?" said Chris, repeating the question for Pete.

Pete thought fast. "The satellites."

The others thought that sounded good, so after the movie they hit the satellites. Knowing what he did about his dad, and fault-tolerance, and encryptors, he decided to keep what he'd overheard a secret. At least until it hit the papers.

THE END

If you'd like to know what Pete does about his dad, and fault-tolerance, and encryptors—and a few things even he doesn't know—turn back and make different choices along the way. Or go to page 151.

The guys looked at each other and knew instantly what they were all thinking—follow Pete!

"Come on!" Chris said. He took off up the stairs and toward the Flight and the Arts exhibit area, the others close on his heels. They couldn't run—there were too many people—but they did manage to walk fast. They weaved through the crowd as fast as they dared, dodging small kids, baby strollers, and glaring adults.

Once in the exhibit area, Sam led them toward the administrative offices.

Meanwhile, Pete took the phone from the receptionist. "Hello?"

"Hello, Pete," said a familiar voice.

"Dad!? What are you calling me here for?"

"First of all, what are you doing at the Air and Space Museum?"

"Looking at exhibits."

"Wrong," he said good-naturedly. "You're walking right into the middle of an FBI sting."

"I am?" he said, a little embarrassed. An FBI sting is when an FBI agent pretends to be a criminal so he can "join" the criminals and find out about their crimes, and so the FBI can catch them red-handed.

"Yeah, and nearly scared the pants off my chief informant."

He must mean Scorpion, thought Pete. He couldn't hold back a smile. "Sorry." Scorpion wasn't an FBI agent. He was an informant, which means he really *was* an assistant in Donations and Acquisitions, but he was telling the FBI things they needed to know.

"That's OK. Say, as long as you're here, how would you like to see a genuine FBI sting come down? I've already cleared it with my captain."

"You mean you're *here,* at the Air and Space Museum?" Pete could hardly believe it. "Sure!"

"It'll mean staying up late and maybe even spending the night."

Just then the guys stormed into the lobby. "Pete, who is it?" blurted out Willy.

He held his hand over the mouthpiece, "It's my dad."

Pete got excited and really wanted to do it, but wasn't sure he wanted to leave the guys. "I don't suppose they could come too?"

"I don't think so. How many?"

"Five."

"Yeah, see that's just too many. I know I can trust you. But I can't vouch for the others. Do what you want, Son. If you'd rather rejoin the guys, that's fine. If you want to join the FBI for an evening, that's fine too." Pete looked at the guys with a torn expression. Have you ever had to choose between two things, both of which you loved? That's what Pete was having to do.

28

CHOICE ⇒

If Pete goes with his dad, turn to page 129.

If he rejoins the gang, turn to page 119.

Sam found himself swept up in everyone else's excitement. *This is neat,* he thought. *Everybody thinks I really know some stuff.*

"As a matter of fact," he said, "I do know about some pretty out-of-the-way places."

Willy reacted right away. "Yes! I knew it!"

Pete was a little more cautious. "Where are they?"

"I can't remember *exactly,*" answered Sam jokingly, trying to be cautious himself by pretending to hold back. "It's been a while, you know. I'm sure once I saw the place again I'd remember. They may have places in the walls behind the exhibits or something." Then he decided to make it a little safer. "Either way, though, it would be tough to get into them with all those people watching."

"What people?" asked Willy.

"You know," moaned Chris, "all the 5 million people looking at the exhibits."

"Oh yeah," said Willy.

"Are you sure they have secret passages in a museum?" continued Pete. "It seems kind of weird."

"Oh yeah!" Sam said as confidently as he could.

"Well, I say we do it," said Chris. "Jim is helping his granddad clean up the church, and this would be the perfect excuse to get him out of it."

This sounded great to everybody, so they hurried

across the Common to Capitol Community Church where Jim's granddad, Mr. Whitehead, was working. He wasn't the pastor or anything like that; he was sort of the jump-starter. The church had been closed for about a year when Mr. Whitehead retired from the mission field several months ago. Now he was trying to reopen the church.

"Hey, Jim, want to go hunting for some more secret passages?" Willy yelled as they bounded up the steps. Jim was just coming out the front door as they approached.

"Sure. I gotta finish up helping my granddad though. It'll be nice and cool under the church after being in this heat."

"No no, this isn't the church," Willy continued. "This is a museum."

"A museum? Where?" They explained their plan. Jim was a little skeptical about the secret passages; he could usually tell when people were exaggerating, and he thought Sam might be. But he kept these thoughts to himself.

"Sounds like fun!" he said. "Let me find out if my grandpa can spare me, though. He's got a lot to do around here." Mr. Whitehead wasn't too happy about letting Jim go. But once the gang promised to spend an hour making up the lost time the next day, he decided it was a perfect arrangement.

Mr. Whitehead's wife, Jean, agreed to take the gang to the subway as long as they had a chaperon. They finally reached Willy's older brother, Clarence (they called him Zeke). By 11:30 they were off, forgetting their lunchtime hunger.

As they rode to the subway station, Sam's thoughts drifted. He felt a little guilty about this secret passages stuff. He felt like he had stumbled into it more than made it up; everybody got excited and he just sort of went along, not wanting to deflate their balloon. But now he was having to cover the original lie with others to keep the thing alive, and *that* was making him nervous. Now he just wanted to get out of it without embarrassing himself massively.

He felt like a bug about to hit a windshield. He could face the windshield and collide bravely into it, admitting to the guys he didn't know about secret passages; or he could dive to the side and try to get everyone to forget about it. He liked diving to the side the most, for it meant minimum humiliation, and minimum humiliation was a big priority.

 **CHOICE**

If Sam takes care of this by admitting it all, turn to page 91.

If he tries to get everyone to forget about it, turn to page 112.

They headed over to the Gemini capsule. Pete was there waiting for them. "When we use our heads, we actually come up with some bright ideas!" said Jim.

They found him more shaken up than they had expected. In fact, he insisted on leaving the museum. *They* could stay. But he insisted on going home.

The other guys sort of automatically rallied to change his mind. They had no idea how strongly he felt because he held back from completely spilling his guts; they were simply upset that some mystery man could so easily ruin Pete's day. "No Scorpion is going to mess with you, Pete, and that's a promise," said Sam. The others nodded and mumbled in agreement.

"Besides," he continued, "*you* talked *me* into coming. And now you're going to cut out? Uh-uh. If I have to suffer, so do you." Pete started to laugh. *That's one of the neat things about Sam,* he thought.

"All for one and one for all, Pete," reminded Chris. "We'll be your bodyguards."

"Yeah!" Willy cheered. He loved this idea. "We'll get glasses to make it official. Anybody messes with you, we're all over their face. You got nothing to worry about, Pete. Come on." He grabbed his arm and started walking.

Willy led them over to the museum shop and found

sunglasses. Everybody got a pair, and a new Secret Service was born.

For the rest of the day, Chris, Sam, Jim, and Willy kept Pete surrounded—just the way the Secret Service does when the president travels. They saw all the exhibits this way. Space Hall, Jet Aviation, Stars, Apollo to the Moon, and Exploring the Planets were their favorites. It got interesting at times, like during a bathroom break and in the Stars exhibit (too dark). But that was just part of the fun. Most important, it took Pete's mind off Scorpion.

They found out about him later anyway.

THE END

Turn back and make different choices along the way, or turn to page 151.

Chris looked at Willy, who was sitting next to Sam, with a sly glance. His eye caught Willy's cup, now empty of root beer and full of melting ice. "Waste him," he said.

Willy grabbed the front of Sam's shirt and pulled, then turned his cup upside down over the opening as Chris and Pete grabbed Sam's hands. Sam yelled and stood as the ice hit his stomach, trying to get loose from the others. He was pretty numb around the belly button by the time they let him go.

"Ahhhh," he sighed happily after he removed the remaining ice cubes from his shirt. "That was cooooolll," he said.

"Yeah, you really loved it," teased Pete.

Just then two guys and two girls walked in, high schoolers the gang recognized from the neighborhood—the kind of thing where they saw each other around but never talked much. The newcomers ordered and smoothly walked over to the Ringers' table.

"What are you kids doing today?" asked Garth. He was in eleventh grade and acted cool. Chris told him of their plans to go to the Air and Space Museum.

"So you're staying behind, huh?" Garth said to Sam. He got a thoughtful look. "Why don't you come with us? We're going to, uh, well," he chuckled and held up a videotape, "see a movie."

"What movie?" asked Sam. Garth held the tape so Sam could see the label. Sam blushed and said he didn't think he should watch that kind of movie.

"Come on, man. Rules are made to be broken. That's my philosophy." The others laughed and nodded their heads.

Chris and Jim looked at Sam. Right then he was really glad to be surrounded by his ice cube terrorists. He wouldn't have wanted to turn down Garth's invitation by himself. This was a lot easier. "No thanks," he said. "I've got other stuff to do."

Garth shrugged. "Suit yourself." Again he held up the tape as he and the others turned to leave. "We're going to *enjoy* our summer vacation."

Once they were gone, Sam shivered. "Gives me the willies."

Willy shivered too, "Gives me the sammies."

Sam poked him, they all laughed, and Willy, Pete, and Chris started heading over to the church to find Jim. Sam stood in the doorway and watched as they walked away. "Bye-bye, boys!" he said in a nasal tone as he waved. "Have a nice ti-ime! Be home by supper, OK?"

THE END
Turn back and see what other choices awaited the Ringers.

"Willy," Sam said, looking him in the eyes, "Jim. Bad man scare Pete. Pete figure out. Guard make Pete disappear into phone twilight zone. Can we go now?"

"Al*riiight,*" they said, just to appease Sam.

Sam led the way at high speed to the Flight and the Arts exhibit area, where he last saw Pete before losing sight of him. Once there, they noticed that it was under construction. Most of the paintings and sculptures were gone, and there were a lot of temporary walls and signs up.

The far east end of the exhibit, though, was what caught Sam's eye. "There," he pointed. Directly ahead of them was a set of double glass doors clearly marked National Air and Space Museum—Administrative Offices.

They went through the doors and stepped up to the receptionist's desk. "Yeah, I saw a guy like that," she said. "He took a phone call at the desk and then was escorted by a guard into the offices."

"What was the call about?" asked Sam.

She looked at him like he'd just proposed marriage. Sam blushed. "I can't tell you *that,*" she said, "but I did get the impression he wasn't coming back." The guys got ultra-attentive. "Said something about spending the night. Looked kind of sad too, like he didn't want to do it. Guess that's parents, huh?"

Chris felt like he was about to explode into a

thousand pieces. "May we go look for him?" he asked in a controlled voice.

"I'm sorry," she said with a sincere look of regret, "but no one is allowed into that area without a pass or escort. Is he a friend of yours?" They nodded, hoping this was some sort of offer to bargain. "Well, if he comes back this way, I'll tell him you're looking for him," she said. "What are your names?"

So much for bargaining. They told her just to tell him the Ringers were looking for him. Then Willy got a thought. "Did the guard come back through?"

"Oh yeah," said the receptionist. "Was carrying a piece of paper, too." *A ransom note!* they said to each other with their eyes.

They thanked her and left the lobby to huddle in the exhibit area. "Well, what do we do now?" asked Jim.

"I say we check out Scorp's office," said Chris. There was a determination in his eyes that surprised the other guys.

"Very funny," said Willy.

"No, I'm serious. Pete is missing. I say we look for him. Sam knows this place. I'm sure we can figure out where Scorp might be hiding him." Chris always wanted to be a hero. He wanted his mom to be proud of him. This chance was just too good to pass up.

"I do?" said Sam jokingly.

"Are you crazy?" said Jim. "This isn't like the old church. The guy could be dangerous. And besides, we shouldn't go snooping around the museum like we own the place. We should call Pete's dad and tell him what happened."

"Why?" asked Willy. "Mr. Andersen already knows about him. Scorp said so himself."

"Besides," Chris jumped in, "the FBI didn't stop Pete from getting kidnapped. And if the guy really is a criminal, he sure isn't going to expect kids to be following him."

Jim thought for a moment. He felt funny about Chris's idea—no matter what they thought had happened to Pete. But he was very insistent, and that made Jim unsure of what to do.

Willy still hadn't decided if he believed Pete had actually been kidnapped. Looking for him would sure be more fun than looking at exhibits, though. And it was obviously important to Sam and Chris. He shook his head as if to clear the clutter. "I'm game either way, Chris. If we're 'all for one and one for all,' then I guess we gotta go for it!"

Sam got chills at the idea of actually finding Scorpion. He wasn't sure anymore that he wanted to find him torturing Pete. But he didn't want to admit he was afraid either—especially when he had led the search this far. And Pete's "phone call" still nagged at him. He agreed to go along with Chris.

Jim was the last to speak.

CHOICE ➤

If Jim decides the gang is right, turn to page 115.

If Jim decides not to go, turn to page 102.

Willy and Clarence actually got along pretty well, despite their teasing. But nobody called him Clarence except his parents. Everybody else called him Zeke.

Zeke was a guy the other members of the gang liked. He was too old to fit into the things they liked to do, but when he was around they didn't mind. Having him be their chaperon actually might work out.

Sam convinced Willy to let him do the asking. "More clout," he reasoned, "since I'm not his brother."

Willy dialed, and Sam adopted his salesman tone. "Zeke! How would you like to have the time of your life?"

"Forget it, Ramirez," Zeke replied.

"But Zeke, it won't cost you anything. This is an all-expense-paid *free trip!* Only an insane man would pass it up."

"I'm insane."

"Zeke," Sam laughed, "we're desperate. We need a chaperon. Preferably an insane chaperon. It's the Air and Space Museum, Zeke. What do you say?"

"Are you sure you want an old man following you all over the place?" This was his way of saying, "I don't want to baby-sit five fourteen-year-old immature kids."

Sam saw it coming. "You can turn us loose once we get there. All you got to do is get us there and make sure we don't break anything. How 'bout it?"

40

Zeke laughed. "Why not? It's summer vacation."

They hung up and, now that they had their chaperon, got permission from their parents. Pete and Sam had to be home by 9:00, Chris by 8:00, and Willy and Zeke by 7:30. Willy's family was leaving at 5:00 the next morning for vacation. The museum closed at 5:30, so they figured they had plenty of time to stay till closing.

Jean took the gang to the station and advised them to spend their money wisely "since the food's expensive."

CHOICE

Turn to page 63.

The gang wasn't too interested in waiting around for forty-five minutes. So they offered a compromise: the gang would pitch in for orange sherbet—Mr. Andersen's favorite—if he would tell all once he got home. Pete's dad said OK.

If he had been totally honest, he wouldn't have done it. Now he wouldn't get home until after nine, making a long day even longer. But he could tell by the looks in their eyes that to be fourteen years old and to come so close to a certified FBI sting operation . . . . Well, how could he refuse?

They called their parents to let them know what was happening, and took off. Their only worry was how Zeke would react when he saw them again. "I think you're the one who's going to get it," said Jim to Sam as they walked.

"Oh yeah?" asked Sam.

"Yeah. *You're* the one who convinced him to come." The Ringers started laughing. Poor Sam. And he hadn't even wanted to come.

"Hey guys, just remember," said Sam nervously, "all for one and one for all. OK?" But they just shook their heads and laughed.

They reached the bottom of the escalator in the Smithsonian subway station and saw Zeke standing there waiting near the fare-card machines.

42

"Hi Zeke," said Willy with a false grin on his face.

"This had better be good," said Zeke with half-serious fury.

"Zeke mah man," said Sam, "it is. It is . . ."

Zeke never laughed so hard again all summer long.

THE END

Turn back and make different choices along the way, or turn to page 151.

Sam was the smallest, so he inched his way between
the boxes and the wall, trying not to make too much noise.
There, as plain as day, three large black cables passed
through a large hole in the wall that was partly covered by
a loose piece of drywall. He returned to whisper this back
to the guys.

Together they moved the boxes as close to either wall
as they could, making space between them for a straight
shot to the hole. "Who's going to go first?" whispered Chris.

"Not me," said Jim.

"Me neither," said Pete.

"Step aside, you mice," said Sam, moving back
toward the hole.

"Not so fast," said Willy, holding him back. "I can
handle this."

"Aw Willy, come on, you always get to plunge into
danger first!"

Willy started to laugh. "Do not."

"Do too," Sam joined in, "and besides, you're going
on vacation, so it's not fair."

"Ouch!" said Jim.

"What happened?" Chris asked, starting to laugh.

"I bumped into the wall," said Jim, himself starting to
laugh. Now they were all laughing.

Sam was the first to recover enough to start crawling

toward the hole. "Last one through has to wash Willy's socks!"

"Aaaargghh!" Instantly it was a mad scramble for the hole like horses bursting from the gate at the races. Sam crawled—or rather was pushed—through and into a stack of empty cardboard boxes, tried to stop but couldn't, ran into a door about three feet into the dark room, and stood up to save himself from getting squashed by the frantic crew pouring in from behind. Willy was last.

In seconds, all five guys were crammed into a small closet. Whatever had been hanging up was now on the floor.

Suddenly Sam remembered the voices and tried frantically to get the others quiet. Before he could even get their attention, Jim decided it was too cramped and got his hand on the doorknob and turned it.

The gang spilled into the next room in a heap of squelched giggling. "Hurmph," said Sam as they landed on top of him. Five heads spun around feverishly, looking for witnesses. They could see none in the darkened room that looked like an average-sized office. The people they had heard before had left the room.

Silence. They stayed quiet for several seconds but could hear nothing. Their hearts were racing.

"Help," said a shallow voice from the bottom.

They untangled themselves and stood, helping Sam to his feet. "My bladder," he whimpered.

They found themselves whispering again. "Guys," said Chris, pointing at the phone on the desk. They looked at each other and knew what they had to decide next.

"What for?" asked Willy. "We still have to get out."

"Yeah, but at least they'd know where we are," answered Chris.

CHOICE

If they call home now, turn to page 88.

If they try to get out first, turn to page 70.

They all got large pops and sat down. Mrs. Whitehead was right; the food was expensive—$3.50 for a large. "They oughta give a discount to people under sixteen," complained Willy.

For the next ten minutes they talked about Pete's mystery man. They wanted to know everything: what he looked like, everything he said, and exactly what happened. Pete filled them in.

Scorpion—that's what they decided to call him, since it sounded neat and "like a hit man," according to Willy—looked just like a million other businessmen: tall, short hair, maybe thirty-five years old, clean shaven, business suit, blah blah blah. Nothing interesting.

Other than what "Scorpion" said to Pete, they didn't have much to go on. Pete caught a few words between when he heard his dad's name and when he turned around, but he couldn't remember them.

As for what happened, he told that story again. The essential facts were: Scorpion said Pete's dad's name, Pete asked him about it, Scorpion recognized Pete, Scorpion clammed up, and Scorpion took off in a huff. That's the way Pete remembered it.

"That's not much to go on," said Chris pessimistically.

"But we also know," added Willy, "that Pete's dad is

an FBI agent who goes after technology thieves. Maybe Scorpion steals space shuttle parts or something."

"Wait a minute," Pete broke in. "I do remember the guy saying 'FBI.' I forgot about that—probably because I just connected it with my dad's name."

The other guys got excited. "Anything else?" asked Chris. "What did he say right before you interrupted him?"

Pete thought hard, rubbing his chin. "Eeeyeaaahh," he said slowly. "He said something. Big word, too. Blah blah something." Pete thought for a moment, then snapped his fingers. "I remember! Something about 'the fault-tolerant encryptor,' ummm, 'Kyle Andersen, with the FBI,' and then something about the 'fault-tolerant encryptor.' That's what the guy said right before I interrupted him."

"Wuh-wuh-wuh-wait a minute, fault-what-what?" said Willy on the edge of his chair, "What's that?"

"You know," said Sam, "Faultallint Descriptor, superhero!"

"Ha ha, very funny," said Willy. Jim broke out in a loud, gargling laugh.

Pete rested the tips of his fingers on his forehead and bowed his head to block out the others and think. "Fault-tolerant encryptor," he muttered to himself. "I read about that somewhere." He looked up. "I think it's a satellite part."

"Huh?" said Chris. The others thought *Huh?* too; they just didn't say it. Pete was the computer person among the Ringers. His idea of a good time was to figure out how to write a program on his home computer or to build an electronic gizmo. He was forever picking up little bits of trivia about technology. Satellites were one of his favorites.

Willy was in shock. "A *satellite part?*" he asked. "You know about *satellites?*"

"Some of us drink from the fountain of knowledge, Willy," said Chris. "Others just gargle."

Suddenly Pete got up from his chair and started walking quickly toward the exit, leaving his chair on its side and the gang in shock. "Come on, guys!" He took off out the exit.

"Wait up!" yelled Willy. "I haven't finished my pop!"

When they finally caught up with Pete, he was walking as fast as he could, weaving his way through the crowd. Jim teasingly scolded him, "Slow down, dude. Where are we going? The satellite exhibit?"

"You got it."

CHOICE

Turn to page 60.

"**W**e're going to break the door down," said Willy.

"Wait a minute, wait a minute," said Pete, "let's think about this first."

"Let's not think about it, let's just do it," said Willy.

"Willy, what if we get in trouble?" Pete asked.

Willy huffed. "The longer we wait, the worse this gets. Zeke is already probably going bananas wondering where we are. If we don't show up pretty soon, he's going to call our parents and then we'll *really* be in trouble." He was sweating. "What do *you* suggest we do—stay here all night?"

"Hey! A sleepover!" said Sam, smiling.

"You punk, this isn't funny," said Willy. "If you hadn't gotten so worked up about secret passages we wouldn't even be in here."

"Wait a minute," said Sam, raising his voice. "*You're* the one who got all worked up about secret passages!"

"I did not!" yelled Willy.

"You did too!" Sam shot back. "'Secret passages? Yes! I *knew* it!'" Sam made a mocking imitation of Willy's excitement at the Freeze earlier in the day.

"Yeah?" said Willy. It was his turn to quote Sam. "'I know some pretty out-of-the-way places.'"

Chris interrupted them, "Guys, would you quit it?

We've got to get out of here. It isn't going to do any good to figure out who's fault it is."

He took a deep breath. "There's got to be something we can do."

"We could set off the alarm," said Sam.

"We could?" asked Jim, surprised.

"Yeah. The motion detectors turn on automatically at nine o'clock. We could wait until then and slide something under the door."

"Nine?" said Willy. "That's more than three hours away!" He glared at Sam.

"Would they find us?" asked Chris.

"They'd know where to look," answered Sam. "And with the light shining under the door, they'd probably figure out where we are. And, we could scream and pound on the door."

"Well if we're going to wait that long, I don't think we should do anything," said Pete, sitting down. "Let's just sit out the night and wait until morning. The place will open up and we'll be able to get out."

Jim said no way to that suggestion. "What would happen to our parents? They would have no idea where we are, they would go completely out of their minds, and when we got home they would peel the skin off us. One way or another, we've got to find some way out of here."

"Guys, I'm sorry, but my family is going on vacation tomorrow, and I'm not waiting around for my parents to think of reasons for leaving me behind to feed the cat," said Willy. "Besides, we're leaving at five o'clock in the morning, and I've got packing to do. Oh man, I'll bet Zeke is having a cow."

"Then let's break the door down," said Chris. "I don't want to get in trouble. *Man,* I do not want to get in trouble. But at least that way we get home as soon as possible."

Sam summarized their situation. "So our options are: get in trouble now, get in trouble a little later, or get in trouble tomorrow morning. Sounds good to me."

"Sheesh," sighed Pete.

CHOICE

If they try to break out now, turn to page 72.

If they decide to set off the alarm or wait out the night, turn to page 13.

Jim decided to follow Pete and motioned excitedly for the others to come along. Chris and Sam looked confused for a second, looked at each other, got frustrated, and then took off after the two runaways.

"Willy, come on!" Chris shouted over his shoulder.

"But I already gave him my ticket!" Willy cried. Very irked, he stepped over the ropes and caught up with the others.

"What? What?" asked Willy, obviously upset at losing his ticket. "Has somebody got diarrhea or something? I already gave the guy my ticket."

Pete didn't have time to explain while they were walking, so Jim clued them in that they were following somebody. They were not too happy with this at first, but the thrill of the chase soon took over. They pretended to notice exhibits and to stroll casually as they kept up with Pete. They had no clue what they were doing, but they were having fun so they forgave him.

Pete led them in the direction they'd gone to reach the theater, up the escalator, past the World War I and Apollo to the Moon exhibits. Then they took a right turn into a short, narrower hallway toward the Flight and the Arts exhibit.

Pete stopped just before entering the exhibit area. The entrance was darker than the center hallway and cluttered with construction stuff. Pete had lost sight of his pursuit when he turned right.

The gang slowed down as Pete inched his way into the exhibit area, peering casually around the corner to the left as he did so. He got there just in time to see a door close across the room. It was marked Authorized Personnel Only.

Pete looked around to make sure he hadn't lost the man in some other direction. No trace of him.

Pete sighed heavily. "He went through that door," he said pointing and a little out of breath.

"I don't think so," said Sam. Everybody ignored him.

"What's the deal, Pete?" asked Willy. "Who were we following?"

Pete told them what had happened in front of the theater.

"What would we have done if we had caught him?" asked Willy.

"We weren't trying to *catch* him," answered Pete. "I just wanted to see where he was going."

"What were you going to do once you found out where he went?" Willy wondered.

"I don't know," he said. "Think about it, guys." He started counting off on his fingers. "One, the guy says my dad's name. Two, he freaks out when he sees me. Three, he says he has no idea who Kyle Andersen is. Four, then he takes off like I've got rabies."

Blank stares. Faces twitching in concentration. "I don't get it," said Jim finally.

"My dad's an FBI agent," Pete replied. "He

investigates technology theft. *This* is the Air and Space Museum."

Chris moaned. "Oh, crud. The guy's a hit man."

Sam couldn't hold back a laugh. "A hit man? No, señor, I don't think so."

"What's a hit man?" asked Jim. No one really knew; they just knew it was bad. Definitely a criminal.

"I just couldn't believe," Pete continued, "someone who knew my dad would act so weird. I mean, this is bizarre. It doesn't compute."

"Are you saying," Jim asked Pete, "that this guy is in trouble with the FBI?"

"Maybe he's just a super-brain," suggested Sam. "You know, one of those antisocial walking technology freaks. Didn't know what to say, so he split."

"You have such a smooth way of describing people, Sam," said Jim sarcastically.

"Whatever," said Willy. "What do we do now? Are we supposed to follow him some more?"

"I don't think he went in therrrre," said Sam again.

"Why not?" the others said at once.

"Because that's an electrical closet."

CHOICE ➡

If they check out the electrical closet, turn to page 133.

If they don't check it out and just assume they lost the man, turn to page 106.

Jim shrugged. "Sounds to me like the guy's legit."

"Then we don't call," said Pete. "Still, we should at least tell my dad about him when we get home."

"Fine," sighed a restless Willy, "we'll tell Mr. Andersen when we get home. Now can we enjoy the museum?"

"We should see Skylab first," said Sam. "That's pretty cool."

"Let's go!" said Jim.

As they started toward the exhibit, Sam pointed out where the telephones were—just in case they changed their minds.

CHOICE

Turn to page 135.

56

The gang decided to go home with Mr. Andersen so they could hear all about what they'd witnessed. They wasted no time starting a friendly interrogation once they were on the road.

"What was all that about, Dad?" asked Pete. The gang huddled around to listen.

Mr. Andersen sighed. "About six months ago the FBI found out that some highly sensitive satellite parts . . ."

"Such as fault-tolerant encryptors?" said Chris carefully. Pete's dad was surprised. "Yes, how did you know?"

"We figured it out," Chris replied.

"*I* figured it out," insisted Pete. "We'll explain after you finish, Dad."

"I hope so," Mr. Andersen replied. "I thought all this was secret. I suppose you figured out the attitude control systems too?" Pete shook his head. "Oh, well, it's nice to know you don't know everything." Sam liked the sound of "attitude control system," so he interrupted and got Pete to explain that it was another important satellite part. Once that was done, Mr. Andersen continued.

"Anyway, these parts, which are crucial to many military satellites, were just disappearing. Nobody knew how or where they were going. We knew there was a Smithsonian Connection, but after that—poof. So we talked to the curator at NASM and zeroed in on Straska—if he saw a fault-tolerant encryptor, he would know what it was."

"Who is he?" asked Willy.

"He's in charge of processing donations and acquisitions. Or at least he *was.*"

"What's that mean?" asked Willy.

"He checks out things the museum gets to see if they can be added to the collection. He's very bright. Has a doctorate in electrical engineering. If he processed one of these stolen parts, no matter what the label said it was, he'd know what it was. There's no way he'd be fooled.

"So we sent one on purpose, just to see what he'd do with it. It arrived today. When Mr. Bluewater and Ms. Peabody, the curator, realized that Straska had seen it but wasn't going to tell them about it, they knew he was the man. So we set up a few bugs and waited to see where he was shipping them. We had an undercover agent working as a guard—Alice, you met her—and with Mr. Bluewater and Mrs. Peabody's cooperation, catching him was going to be a piece of cake."

"Then we showed up," said Jim, smiling.

"Then you showed up," repeated Mr. Andersen. "Don't do that again, OK?" he said in jest. "When we heard you guys, at first we didn't know what was going on. Then we heard Pete identify himself, and we just chucked our plans and moved in."

"I still don't understand," said Jim. "If this Straska guy's so bright, why steal this stuff and sell it to . . . geeks?"

"Bright doesn't mean wise, Jim. It just means he didn't have to work very hard to figure things out. That's different from making good choices. To this guy, rules are made to be broken. That's what happens when you have no respect for God."

"Is he going to jail?" asked Jim.

"That's for the court to decide," said Mr. Andersen.

"But isn't he guilty?"

"That's for the court to decide," repeated Mr. Andersen. "All we do is gather evidence."

This seemed strange to the guys, but they accepted it anyway.

Finally Sam couldn't resist any longer. He grabbed Willy by the collar and looked into his face, "Son, maybe we can find a replacement around here for your attitude control system."

Willy started laughing and waving his hand, "Phew, back off, encryptor breath." Everybody laughed.

"Speaking of attitude control systems," said Mr. Andersen, "mine could use some fuel. Want to stop and get pizza? I'm headed for a late dinner anyway, and you guys must be starving."

A virtual riot broke out. "Where did you get this guy?" said Chris to Pete.

"Ah, found him somewhere," said Pete, smiling.

THE END

Turn back and make different choices along the way, or turn to page 151.

Sam really didn't want to go to the museum. He had been there so many times. Betty noticed how long he was taking to answer.

"I don't think Sam really wants to go," she said.

Sam didn't say anything, just gave them a look that said, "She's right." He hated to spoil their fun, but he felt like he had no choice. Even ice cream gets sickening when you eat too much of it.

The other boys were a little frustrated. They wanted to go, and they didn't want to give up on the idea just because Sam did. They wished he would change his mind, but they didn't think he would.

Sam felt bad. "I'm sorry, guys," he said. "Going would kind of be like taking summer school."

CHOICE

If they still try to convince Sam to go, turn to page 140.

If they decide to go without him, turn to page 127.

Pete led them to the first floor Looking at Earth exhibit where all the satellites were. He had been mesmerized by them even back when he had come here in second grade.

He parked himself near the entrance of the exhibit area and pointed at a satellite hanging from the ceiling. "Guys, the fault-tolerant encryptor is something electronic that goes in communications satellites—something very few people, except aerospace engineers and techno freaks, would know about." Pete was so excited he was nearly out of breath.

"What is it?" asked Chris.

"It's an encryptor," answered Pete. "It puts signals in code."

"What signals?" asked Jim.

"The signals that pass through the satellite," answered Pete. They thought for a moment but still didn't get it. "A communication satellite is sort of like a cutoff man," explained Pete, using a baseball analogy. "A transmitter on the ground sends signals up into the sky, the satellite picks them up and sends them back down to a receiving station."

"And the encryptor," added Willy, "messes up the signal before sending it back down . . ."

". . . so no one can receive the message without an *un*encryptor," finished Jim.

"Exactly," said Pete. "But the real heavy part is the

fault-tolerant part. See, out in space these satellites take a pounding from space junk like ions and particles and . . . I don't understand all of it, but basically they gotta be real tough—like earthquake proof. They call it 'space-qualified.' Anyway, a lot of those terrorist countries don't know how to make fault-tolerant electronics yet, and they'd love to get their little pawsies on them."

"So fault-tolerant plus encryptor equals hot item," said Sam, tripping over all the syllables.

"You got it," said Pete.

"Whoa," said Chris.

"Wait a minute," said Willy. "What's the big deal? This is a space museum. What's so weird about them getting a fault-whatever encryptor satellite part?"

"The FBI—and Scorp's reaction," said Pete.

"Oh yeah," said Willy.

Jim cleared his throat and asked sheepishly, "What exactly is the FBI?"

"They investigate big crime," said Sam grandly. Jim looked at Pete for confirmation.

"That's the general idea," said Pete.

"Which means," thought Chris out loud, "Scorpion's in a heap of trouble." Pete nodded.

"Awesome!" said Willy.

There was one of those silences in which everyone in the group gets chills at the same time. Whoever they met in front of the theater was not Mr. Rogers. Now they were talking about crime, terrorists, and high tech equipment. They didn't know whether to be scared or excited.

O Lord, Jim thought, *please protect us.* Willy and Chris

were praying along the same lines. Miss Whitehead had reminded her class so many times that it's the little prayers that help us learn to pray the big prayers. Willy and Chris had learned they could pray about anything and everything.

Just then their prayers were interrupted by a hauntingly familiar voice. "I'm glad I bumped into you again, Mr. Andersen."

They all turned. It was Scorpion.

Scorpion fit perfectly the description Pete gave, except that he had no scowl, just a warm and friendly smile. He didn't look nearly as mean as they had imagined him. Pete could hardly believe it.

Scorpion grinned and held out his hand to Pete.

CHOICE

If Pete runs, turn to page 107.

If Pete shakes Scorpion's hand, turn to page 18.

The gang arrived at the museum at around one o'clock, thirsty and grateful for air-conditioning, but too fascinated to care. The first thing they entered was a huge room with dozens of people milling about and looking at flight stuff. The ceiling went the full height of the building, so they could see a second floor balcony toward the center. Hanging from the ceiling high overhead was a very old-looking biplane. Two space capsules were displayed in the middle of the floor. Against the walls were model rockets and jets, some behind Plexiglas windows and others behind thick red ropes clipped to portable poles. Two wide hallways led away to the left and right from the center of each wall. There were exhibits everywhere.

The whole building was laid out a lot like a gigantic two-story animal barn, with a wide center "hallway" and cubicles on either side. Most of the exhibits were in the cubicles, which were actually huge rooms, but the hallway part held some of them too.

"This is nothing compared to what it's like on a Saturday," Sam observed. "Packed in here like sardines."

"What should we see first, Sam?" asked Jim.

"I don't know. What do you want to see?" answered Sam.

Pete cocked his head. "Didn't we have this conversation already?"

"Hold it just a minute," said Zeke. "Before we do anything, we need to decide on a place to meet when you're ready to leave." They decided to use the Gemini capsule as their home base. They'd meet there at 5:15 when they were ready to leave or in case anyone got separated from the group. With that settled and a warning not to break anything, Zeke went off by himself.

The theater entrance was only a few yards away on their left, so the gang went over to check it out. "Hmmm," observed Pete, "showings at 1:30, 3:00, 5:30, and 7:00. It's 1:10 now. Should we wait?"

"I suggest," said a woman's voice from behind them, "that you get in line now if you want the good seats." They turned around to see a short, plain-looking woman with glasses. She was dressed in a business suit and smiling like she knew what she was talking about. She was alone. "By 1:15 this line will be fifty people long, so I suggest you get in now," she continued.

The gang looked at each other awkwardly. "Thanks," Jim said, smiling back. He tended to be a bit more polite than the rest of the guys. He led the way over to the line. "Come on, guys." They got their tickets, got in line, and waited. By 1:20 there was a line stretching back so far that it curved around to the left side. They were glad they had taken the woman's advice.

While they waited, Sam gave them the scoop on what was worth seeing and what wasn't. (Even though he didn't enjoy coming to see the exhibits for himself, he liked sharing his knowledge. It made him feel important.) "The kite shop's pretty neat," he said. "But everything in there's pretty expensive. The history of flight exhibits are pitsville—forget those. You can see where most of the space stuff is over where the line curves around—that's pretty neat," he said, pointing. "That's Skylab. Over next to the . . ."

Sam kept talking, but Pete's attention was interrupted by the sound of someone saying his dad's name. Startled, he turned around. He saw a tall, serious-looking man talking to the woman in glasses. He was wearing a dark business suit and a disgusted scowl on his face. It was the man he had heard. They didn't notice Pete.

CHOICE

If Pete asks the man about this, turn to page 82.

If Pete just listens, turn to page 24.

Willy never skipped a beat and the others followed, Sam included.

They went up the escalator and around the second floor, winding through the exhibits like a centipede. After a while, the arms added gentle wave motions, which drew many stares. Several adults glared at them, and they were looked over by more than one guard. But they weren't running, getting in anyone's way, making noise, or touching anything—and that pretty much satisfied most adults. Some even laughed.

As the gang entered the Flight and the Arts exhibit, they noticed that most of it was shut down for remodeling. They hadn't seen this before because they had avoided it altogether. There were lots of temporary walls and signs saying Pardon Our Dust. It was pretty messy, and the exhibit area was completely empty of visitors and guards.

It was then that Sam made a snap decision.

Back at the Gemini capsule, Zeke looked at his watch. It was 5:25. He watched as people streamed out the revolving doors.

Sam led them behind one of the partitions and into what he thought was an unmarked broom closet, but which was actually marked Authorized Personnel Only. Once everyone was in, he quietly closed the door and turned on the light. The room was about five feet wide by fifteen feet deep. He was surprised to find it empty except for a large humming electrical panel and two huge metal boxes on wheels shoved all the way to the back.

"Ta-daaaa!" Sam spread his arms.

"What's this?" asked Jim.

"A confessional booth," replied Sam.

Chris laughed automatically without really understanding.

"Guys, I wanted to tell you something," said Sam, "but I didn't want to tell you in public, and I *especially* didn't want to tell you in front of Zeke." He took a deep breath. "Remember the secret passage I was going to show you?"

"Oh yeah!" Willy started looking around. They had forgotten about it.

"Well, the actual chance of me showing you a secret passage is something like one in four hundred thousand kajillion with about thirty-nine extra zeros."

Willy looked confused.

Jim didn't. "You mean there are no secret passages?" he said.

"Not," replied Sam, "in the known universe of this building. That I know of."

Willy looked disappointed. Pete was poking around the metal boxes. Chris was conscious of the time and stayed near the door.

Sam looked at Willy. "I'm sorry, buddy. Everybody got excited about it back at the Freeze, and I just—I don't know."

"You should have just told us," said Willy. "It would have been OK."

"Yeah," added Jim. "We would have had a good time. Shoot, we *did* have a good time!"

"I know," Sam replied, "but I—"

"I hate to interrupt our little party here, gentlemen," said Chris, looking at his watch, "but it's five-thirty."

"Oh," said Sam. "Guess we better get out of here."

Chris turned the doorknob and pushed on the door, but it wouldn't budge. After several tries, he said, "Hey, it won't open!"

"Oh no," Sam said, taking over at the doorknob.

"What?" said Willy nervously, starting to sweat. He was claustrophobic.

"Looks like we're locked in."

"How?" asked Pete.

"I don't know," replied Sam, working on the door.

"You mean we're locked in?" asked Willy.

"It looks that way," replied Sam, giving up on the door.

"Oh crud," Willy said, working at the doorknob himself.

"What do we do now?" asked Jim.

"Don't ask me," said Pete.

When the guys hadn't showed by 5:30, Zeke left the building by the north entrance with the last of the visitors. He wasn't worried about the gang at all; in fact, he was sure they were playing a trick on him—hiding in the bushes or something like that so they could watch him panic. It was just the kind of thing they would do. Well, he wasn't going to give them the satisfaction . . .

Every one of the guys worked on the door, but it wouldn't budge.

"We're going to be in *massive* trouble," said Pete.

"Our parents are going to go nuts," added Chris, looking for ways to pick the lock.

"And then they're going to *kill* us," continued Pete.

"And *then* they'll ground us for ten years," said Sam.

"Not to mention getting in trouble with the museum," added Jim.

"Guys, this door isn't budging," concluded Chris.

"What are we going to do?" asked Jim again.

CHOICE

If they pound on the door as loudly as they can, turn to page 142.

If they talk about what to do first, turn to page 49.

There was a door on the right and a door on the left. The door on the left was solid. The door on the right had one of those cloudy windows in it.

They figured the door on the right was the way out, so they tried it first. At the last second they realized there was somebody standing right outside. Since they weren't too eager to attract attention, they pulled back.

"Let's try the other one first," whispered Chris. They moved quietly over to the other side of the room.

Jim opened the door and peeked through, and the others followed. They found themselves in what could only be described as a very large, very cluttered attic. Work benches and stools, things Pete recognized as complicated electronic testers, filing cabinets, movable walls, high-tech–looking gadgets, model aircraft, and stuff of all kinds was littered everywhere. A few overhead lights gave it a dusty glow.

"This is worse than Zeke's room," whispered Willy.

Suddenly a loud, piercing bell started ringing. They froze in terror. They had set off an alarm! They instinctively ran for the closet they had wanted so badly to get out of.

They never made it. A guard had immediately entered the office from the other door and turned on the lights.

"Stop right there!" he ordered. Again they froze.

"I don't wanna die," said Sam.

The guard told them to face the wall and not to move. He spoke into a walkie-talkie, and soon the alarm was off. Their ears were ringing.

"Gives new meaning to the word *Ringers,* doesn't it?" Pete said below his breath.

"Be quiet," said the guard roughly. Two others arrived, told the guys to explain, and called their parents. Within a half an hour, the gang was free.

For the most part, the parents were pretty fair about it. They grounded the whole bunch. Jim's granddad sort of bailed them out: They could do part of their time helping him clean and fix up the church. The parents figured the hard work would be good for them (you know how parents are); Mr. Whitehead figured that he could use the help; and the guys figured they'd rather do that than sit around all day.

As far as punishment goes, this actually wasn't so bad. Jim's granddad was a neat man to talk to. They got to do something useful, which made them feel good. And they got to be with each other. That's not such a bad combination.

Besides, you know what happens when the Ringers get together. . . .

THE END

If you haven't met Victor yet, turn back and make different choices along the way.

The fact that none of them had ever broken a door down before led to a lively discussion about how to do it. Willy wanted to kick it, Sam wanted to push it, Chris wanted to barrel into it with his shoulder, and Pete wanted to pry it open with a crowbar. In the end, they figured they'd seen more door-kicking than door-shouldering or door-pushing on TV, so that must mean door-kicking was best. At least that's how they did it on cop shows. They didn't have a crowbar, so prying was out anyway.

Willy kicked first. It did nothing to the door and gave him a nasty throb in his heel.

"Let me try," said Pete.

"No no," Willy insisted, "I can get it." He leaped from his feet and kicked with both at once, nearly landing him flat on his back and beheading Jim with his flying elbow in the process. They picked him up and dusted him off. The door was seated squarely in place.

"Maybe if two of us try at once," said Willy. The rest of them were ready to give up, but they tried one more time. It was no use. They were just bruising their feet.

"Oh well," said Sam, "it would have cost half a year of paper route money to replace anyway."

"Why don't we just pound on the door?" said Jim. "Some guard is bound to hear us, and we won't have to wait until nine o'clock to set off the alarm!"

They looked at each other like people do when they're thinking, *Why didn't we think of this before?*

"The man's a genius," said Sam.

Sometimes good ideas don't come until you've tried the bad ones.

 **CHOICE**

Turn to page 142.

The boys were laughing as they left the Freeze and headed over to the church. They found Jim and then called their parents and got permission to go. Willy was reminded that his family would be leaving on vacation the next day at 5:00 A.M. That meant they had to be back by 7:30 at the absolute latest. But that left plenty of time after the museum's 5:30 closing time. So they double-checked their cash supply and headed out.

The walk to Ballston station took about a half hour and four T-shirts of sweat. "I will never get used to this," complained Willy of the weather.

Jim smiled. "Then you'd better stay out of the Amazon Basin."

"I'll see what I can do," Willy replied. The trip down the escalator, down to the subway station where it's always cool and dry, restored all attitudes to normal.

"So what's at this Air and Space Museum?" asked Jim as they got on the train. The conversation that followed is just too embarrassing to print. Jim's three companions tried to sound like expert Washingtonians, veterans of a hundred visits to each and every sight in the city with detailed knowledge of every floor plan. But people who live there are often the worst about seeing sights, and this crew was no exception. Before long it was obvious to Jim that they didn't know what they were talking about. They changed the subject.

"Do you think we'll get to Mars by the year 2000 like the president said we will?" asked Pete.

"Are you kidding?" said Chris. "Look how much they keep messing up the space shuttle. And it costs a million billion dollars every time. Forget it."

"That's what they said about the moon, but they got there," said Willy. "I think we'll make it."

Pete and Jim said you can't know the future anyway, so why sweat it?

It was this debate that made them end up at what Jim mistook for the museum. "Is this it?" Jim asked, but his words were interrupted by the announcement, "This isssss . . . Nationallll Airrrrrport," as they pulled into another station.

The others looked around. "Uh-oh," said Chris. Jim was looking at the map.

"Uh-oh what?" asked Pete.

"This is National Airport," said Willy.

"Derrrr," said Jim, "no kidding. But is this it?"

"Afraid not," said Chris, pointing to a dot on the map. "We want Smithsonian . . . here. This is National Airport . . . here." They were at least a half dozen stations past their stop.

"Forget the Air and Space Museum," said Willy. "Let's watch planes!"

Chris looked at Jim. "It's OK with me," Jim answered. "I thought it was the museum anyway." With that slight change in plans unanimously approved, they exited the subway and sauntered over to the terminals.

As it turned out, they soon regretted their mistake. They went to the observation deck, browsed in the gift shop, and stared out the window at planes. But to their surprise, this all got boring quickly. After a while all the planes looked the same, and the crowds and security guards hostile to summer-vacationing fourteen-year-olds seemed to put out a mat that said, "*Go away.*" By three o'clock they were gagging on stale airport fumes, and at Pete's suggestion they left.

"The airport always reminds me of Brazil," said Jim as he slumped down in the orange bench seat of the subway train, facing backward.

"How's that?" asked Willy.

"That's how we get there and back," came the reply. "I miss it." His face became thoughtful as the others almost automatically got quiet. It was strange to them to think of missing another country.

Just then it came to Pete's mind that Jim hadn't really talked much about Brazil, even though he'd grown up there, and he wondered why. "What is it like?" he asked.

"What do you mean?" said Jim.

"You know. Like what are kids our age like? What do they do? Do they act like us?" The others laughed.

Jim thought for a moment. "Well," he began, then leaned forward and started telling stories without periods. As he waved his arms and talked nonstop, the guys learned about things they'd never seen and sounds they'd never heard. It was all so different from what they'd known in tiny little Millersburg. It made them glad that Jim and his sister, Tina, had come, yet they were a little sad that they themselves would never see this other part of the world. Of course, there was no way they could know then about the chance that was about to come—and sooner than even Jim and Tina would have expected.

The Freeze was in sight by 4:15. Right before they reached the sidewalk in front, Willy suddenly got an idea and frantically motioned for them to join him around the corner where they couldn't see the entrance. "Guys, I got an idea."

"Sam, would you come out here please!" Betty called out a few minutes later.

Sam emerged from the freezer in back. "What's up?"

"Would you help me move this malt machine? I've got to get it a little closer to this drain, and it's too heavy to lift by myself."

"Sure." He helped her, she said thanks, and Sam headed back to his cold work.

In the meantime, several familiar figures had snuck past them and into the freezer. Sam received a shocking and unexpected reception as he opened the door.

"*Aaaahhhhh!*" yelled the gang, indulging in the thrill of an ambush. Sam responded in kind, driven to scream at the top of his lungs with the uncontrollable terror that only a bona fide, truly scared person is capable of. The noise was so intense that Betty held her ears.

Sam half turned to run, then changed his mind in midscream to wail at his tormentors, "*Aaaaahhhhh* you guys are going to *diiiiiiiiieeeee!*" while they pointed at him the way guys do at soccer games when they mean "in your face" and then collapsed in a heap of laughter.

Betty just stood there shaking her head. "You guys are bad for business."

It was a day none of them would forget.

THE END

Turn back and make different choices along the way. See what other adventures the Ringers *could* have had! Or turn to page 151.

They decided that the FBI wouldn't do anything even if they called. It was too early. Zeke's search plan sounded good anyway, and so they plotted. They got a brochure and map for everybody then divvied up the museum.

They agreed to meet back at the Gemini capsule in half an hour, which would be about four-forty-five.

They looked everywhere—the exhibit areas, the gift shop, the kite shop, the cafeteria, even the rest rooms. They asked guards. They checked Lost and Found.

It was like looking for a needle in a haystack. When they met back at the Gemini capsule, they were tired and frustrated. It was obvious they were never going to find Pete. And they were starving.

They sat down at the Gemini capsule like a set of third-generation Raggedy Andys. Some were rubbing their eyes. Some were staring into space. Some were staring at their eyelids.

"Do they take messages at the security desk?" Jim asked Sam.

"Bo Diddly!" said Sam, "I completely forgot about that! Yeah, they do."

Willy looked at Sam with eyes of vengeance. "You forgot? You mean there could be a message from Pete right now at the security desk explaining everything? You mean we have been—"

"OK, OK, I'll go check." Sam lifted his tired body off the bench and trudged across the echoing exhibit hall.

"If he's OK, I'm going to strangle him," said Willy.

"Who, Sam or Pete?" asked Chris.

"Pete."

Jim chuckled. "He's doomed, then. Either Scorp tortures him, or we do."

"Yeah," Chris agreed. "Either way, I'd hate to be Pete right now."

"I'd hate to be Pete, period," said Zeke.

"I wish you were," said Willy. "Things around the house would be a lot more tolerable."

"You're going down, boy," said Zeke.

Willy sneered.

Chris watched the Ringers' unofficial court jester as he shuffled back toward them from the security desk. "He's doomed." Sam was carrying a piece of paper in his hand.

Sam cleared his throat and read from the three-by-five card. "Ahem. 'I ran into my dad, and I'll be going home with him. I'll have to explain later. Have a great time. Pete. P.S. Willy and Zeke—see you in a week.'"

"Told you so," said Zeke.

"He's doomed," said Willy.

Tired, grumpy, frustrated, hungry, and ready to strangle Pete, they made their way to the revolving doors, in a sort of unspoken agreement that it was time to leave.

THE END

If you're still wondering who Scorpion is and what
happened to Pete, turn to page 26. Or turn back and
make different decisions along the way. Or turn to page
151.

"**E**xcuse me," Pete said awkwardly, interrupting the two. The man jumped, which startled Pete. "I-I heard you say my dad's name—I think. Do you know Kyle Andersen?" he asked.

The man gulped the way you do when trying to hold back a gasp. Pete had caught him off guard for some reason.

A little embarrassed and a little scared, Pete shivered. *What did I say?* he thought. He didn't like making tall strangers nervous.

The man tried to compose himself, but his face showed a scowl instead. "I beg your pardon?" he asked angrily. Yep, this man was not only scowling, he was mad and surprised too. He was trying to hide it but not having much success.

Pete was getting very uncomfortable and sweating like mad, but he kept going. "Maybe you know him from church—Kyle Andersen? Looks a lot like me, except he's taller and has less hair?"

Jim noticed that Pete was talking to the man instead of listening to Sam. He tuned his ear to listen.

The man just stared. "No," he said coolly. "I don't believe so."

Pete shivered again. Did he mean no, he didn't know Pete's dad, or no, he didn't know him *from church?* Who was he? He definitely said, "Kyle Andersen." Of course, it could be another Kyle Andersen. But then why did the man say . . .

Wait a minute . . .

"Excuse me," the man growled, turned, and walked away quickly.

Pete suddenly got an awful feeling in the pit of his stomach. *Who around here would know my dad and lie about it?* It was not really a question. Pete knew the answer. *Oh, I should never have opened my mouth.*

He turned to Jim, afraid to look the woman in the eye, then back at the man walking quickly away, then back at Jim, then back . . .

"Guys—," he started to say but was interrupted.

"Please step forward and present your tickets," said a voice near the front of the theater. It was 1:25. They were letting people in. Willy was next in line. There was no time to explain—if he was going to follow the man, he would have to just do it.

Pete started to do some serious sweating.

CHOICE

If Pete follows the man, turn to page 148.

If he goes into the theater with the guys to explain what happened, turn to page 10.

"They've got a new movie at the museum theater too," added Betty. "It's about manned missions to Mars, I think."

"Neato!" cried Willy.

"Sounds good, Sam," said Chris enthusiastically. "Whadda ya say?"

"Alright, you've got me," Sam said with another wag of his spoon. "If I get bored with the exhibits I can just look at you guys."

They all jabbed him teasingly and laughed, then walked across the Common to Capitol Community Church to ask Jim's granddad, Leonard Whitehead, for a ride. The church was where they got their name, the "Ringers." It was from a saying Miss Whitehead, their Sunday school teacher, had written on the board: "Remember to be Ringers!" This was her way of encouraging the boys to be like Christ. Also, Miss Whitehead's brother, Mr. Whitehead, who was trying to reopen the church after it had closed over a year before, had recruited the gang to ring the bell at certain traditional times of the day. You might say they stumbled into it. But that's another story.

Mr. Whitehead was cleaning up in the church office. "Hey, Mr. Whitehead!" Chris called out. The others echoed the greeting as they trailed in behind. "Is Jim around?"

"Yeah, he's up in the bell tower sweeping up. Should be down pretty soon, though. It's hot up there."

"It's hot down here, too." Chris turned to the others, "Let's go rescue him, guys."

"To the rescue!" cried Willy.

"Ho!" said Pete.

"Back, vile heat!" cried Sam.

Together they dashed to the front of the church, where the secret stairway to the bell tower opened to the ground floor foyer. Jim had left it open. They climbed the stairs, making the two sharp left turns, dripping sweat as they went. When they reached the top of the stairs they could hardly believe how hot it was up there.

Jim was holding a broom in one hand and a tall glass of lemonade in the other. He had heard them coming. "Hi, guys. Want to help?" He held out the broom.

A small chorus of "Give me a break!" "You've got to be crazy!" and "Right!" erupted from the sweating quartet.

"Nay, fair maiden, we've come to rescue thee from the vile heat and humidity of yon bell furnace!" cried Sam. Everyone laughed.

"How'd you like to go to the Air and Space Museum?" asked Willy.

"The Hair in Space Museum?"

"The *Air and Space* Museum," Willy corrected him. "It's a really neat place, and it's air-conditioned. Want to go?"

Jim just looked at them. He had grown up as a missionary kid in Brazil and had been in the Washington area only a few weeks. He wasn't familiar with the sites so familiar to the "natives." Finally he agreed, "Sure, I guess so. Let me ask my grandpa."

They all scampered down the stairs and back to the office where Mr. Whitehead was working, being careful to close the door to the bell tower that only they and Mr. Whitehead knew about. The church wasn't air-conditioned, and the boys could hardly believe someone of retirement age like Mr. Whitehead could work in that heat. Yet there he was, cleaning and repairing the historic old building. Several of the boys noticed how much he reminded them of Miss Whitehead, his twin sister.

They told Jim's granddad of their plan, but he was hesitant to let Jim go with so much work to do. A promise by the whole gang to make it up the next day convinced him it would be alright.

The only thing they needed now was a ride. "Maybe Jean can take you," said Mr. Whitehead, picking up the phone and calling his wife. After talking a few minutes, he put down the receiver. "She can take you. But you'll have to get permission from your parents first, and she won't take you unless you have a chaperon."

"A *chaperon?*" they all groaned at once.

"Yep."

"Who?" asked Pete.

"Well, somebody. You'll have to find somebody."

They stood around for a few seconds, a little deflated. Who could they ask to chaperon them who wouldn't spoil the fun? They narrowed it down to two possibilities: Willy's older brother and Chris's older sister.

CHOICE

If they ask Willy's older brother, turn to page 39.

If they ask Chris's older sister, turn to page 126.

They decided to call home. It was 7:15. Even though their parents probably weren't as overcome with panic as they would be if it were 11:15, surely Zeke would have called them by now and told them they were missing.

There was enough light coming through the translucent window in the door for Willy to dial. They decided he should call first since Zeke was their chaperon.

Once on the line with his mom, he explained what had happened and where they were. "We're OK and we're coming home," he said, hoping that would be it and they'd get out without any more fanfare.

"You wait just one minute, William George Washington," she said sternly. This meant trouble. "You aren't going *anywhere*. You're staying right where you are, and you're going to call Security."

"Security? But then we'll get in trouble!"

"You're *already* in trouble, young man."

"Why?"

"What do you mean *why?* You were supposed to meet Clarence at 5:15, not go snooping around closets where you got no business being. Now if you don't call Security and get your hide out of there without setting off a hundred alarms, you're going to be in more trouble with us than you already are with Clarence."

"Zeke is . . . mad?"

"No, he's just tickled pink that you made him wait in the heat for two hours with no idea where you were. If I hadn't told him to wait for you, he'd have abandoned you by now."

"He's still waiting out front?"

"I *just* told him to come home."

"Oh."

"And you'd better call Pete's mom right away. She's all upset for some reason."

"OK, Mom."

"Alright. Do you guys need anything to get home? You got fare cards and all that?" Willy said yes and hung up.

The others didn't need to ask how the call went.

The call to Pete's mom went a lot like Willy's.

They were soon on the phone to Security. They found the number on the desk. Once they had a chance to think about it, they felt better involving the authorities anyway.

The two guards who came surveyed the gang and shook their heads, mumbling something about this room getting all the action tonight. They listened to the gang's story, took down their names and numbers, and called everyone's parents to make sure they knew where they were. After a few stern warnings about staying out of unauthorized areas, the guards let the whole crew use the bathroom and then led them to a side emergency exit. By 7:45 the Ringers were outside in the hot, humid D.C. air.

It almost felt better than the air-conditioning.

THE END

If you haven't figured out yet what the Smithsonian
Connection is, turn back and make different choices
along the way.

Sam decided he didn't want to keep hiding from the guys. He cleared his throat. This was not going to be easy.

"Guys, I have a confession to make." He glanced around at them sheepishly and waited, hoping for some sign that they wouldn't remove his teeth when they found out. "I don't really know about any secret passages in the museum. All I know about are broom closets, and maybe where the security room is. But other than that, mops are as secret as I get. Please don't kill me."

They were all tense for a moment. It wasn't that they were mad at Sam. It was just that they weren't sure what to do. They waited to make sure he was finished.

Finally Chris said, "It's OK, buddy."

"Yeah, don't let it hack you," said Willy.

Sam nodded. "Thanks."

"What's that verse about friends . . . oh, I can't remember . . . " said Chris.

"The one we learned back in seventh grade Sunday school?" asked Willy.

"Yeah," said Chris. "'Friends love . . . all the time,' and something . . . something . . ."

"There's something in there about ad-something too," said Willy. "*Adversary,* that's it. 'Friends love all the time, . . . and even when they're adversaries too'!" He smiled. "Or something like that."

Pete laughed. "'Friends love all the time, and also when there's *adversity,*' is more like it."

Jim said coolly, "'Friends love all the time, and a brother is born for adversity'?"

"Yeah, that's it!" said Chris.

"No! No! I've got it!" cried Willy. "'*A* friend loves at all times, and a brother is born for adversity'!"

Jim leaned back and folded his hands behind his head. "Proverbs 17:17."

"Ringers *recite it!*" jammed Willy.

"All for one and one for all!" said Chris in a mock French accent, standing.

"Ho!"

"Ho!"

"Ho!"

"Ho!"

They gave each other high fives and headed for the museum.

At this point, it didn't really matter if Sam had come clean at first or eventually. The confession made him feel much better about the trip. He could stop sweating. And if they had fun it would be because the Ringers were together, not because they were chasing a secret passage that didn't exist.

They knew that just being together would be an adventure.

Turn to page 63.

Most of the guys were too awake to think about a nap, so they said nothing, and eventually the conversation turned to the boxes. "What do you suppose is in them?" asked Sam.

"That's what I've been trying to figure out," replied Pete. "They look like huge toolboxes to me."

"Maybe this is a Sears outlet store," said Sam.

"They're not ordinary boxes, that's for sure," Pete continued, ignoring Sam. He searched the edges looking for openings or other telltale clues but found nothing. Tapping on them gave a hollow gonglike sound in some places; solid in others.

"Shake one," said Willy.

Pete grabbed the end of the one closest to him and tried to lift it but couldn't. He shrugged his shoulders.

"Maybe it's artwork," suggested Chris. That made sense. This was, after all, the Flight and the Arts exhibit.

Just then Pete noticed, by looking between them, a loose piece of drywall leaning against the back wall; he squirmed his way back there and pulled at it. "Bonanza!"

"What? What?" asked several of the others.

"A hole in the wall!" said Pete. He peered into it while the others scampered over to see. It was not a good angle for any of them, including Pete, so he backed out and they together shifted the boxes to make a straight shot between them to the hole.

"May I take back what I said about secret passages?" said a grinning Sam.

"Hey," said Willy, poking everybody, "didn't I say there were secret passages? I told you there were secret passages!"

The wall itself was hollow, about six inches thick, made of metal studs and drywall. A hole of similar size had been cut through the other side of the wall, and through it passed three large black cables leading to the electrical panel.

"This is a very positive development," said Sam. Setting off the alarm had never really seemed like the best option, just the least painful.

This changed everything. If the hole led somewhere, they might be able to get out of the museum without alerting the National Guard in the process.

"Wait a minute," said Pete, "what if we run into somebody?"

"Then we'll be careful not to knock them over," answered Sam. "Unless it's a girl, in which case we—"

Willy gave Sam a friendly punch in the arm.

Since Pete found the hole, they elected him to go first. The normally cautious recruit looked back at his companions and licked his lips nervously.

"Sic 'em, Zorro," said Sam, right behind Willy, who was right behind Pete.

Pete sighed and crawled into the darkness slowly. About three feet into the room, he saw that the three cables passed through the wall on the right, but through a much smaller hole. Ahead of him was a door; he could see light at the bottom.

Pete stood up. Several coat hangers sang their tune. He was in a closet. It was small, with only a few boxes, a sweater and some other clothes hanging up, and about a half dozen unused metal coat hangers.

Willy was right behind him. "Wait," Pete whispered. "It's a closet. Go back."

Willy balked.

"Go back," Pete insisted.

"Just tell me what the deal is, and I'll pass it on," said Willy.

"There's not enough room in here for all of us," said Pete.

"Can't you get the door open?" asked Willy.

"I haven't tried it yet."

"Well, if you open the door, maybe there *will* be enough room for us."

"But what if we run into somebody? I think I hear machines or something."

"Say hi. I don't know—just do something."

Pete sighed heavily. "OK."

Without really wanting to, he opened the door and looked through.

The first thing he saw was a man sitting at a desk about six feet away. He spun his chair around and looked at Pete with a shocked expression on his face. He had been typing at a laptop computer. Beside him on the floor was a large box with a Federal Express sticker on it.

"Hi," said Pete.

"Who are you?" the man asked angrily, looking around nervously. "What are you doing in here?"

CHOICE

Turn to page 144.

Willy was getting tired of doing everything *except* seeing exhibits. Jim was convinced it was nothing. Chris figured it was either totally safe or something serious at home—in either case, it made sense to wait a little longer before jumping to conclusions. Chris, Jim, and Willy went through Skylab to kill time while Sam waited for Pete.

They were surprised to find Sam still alone when they emerged. "Still no Pete?" Jim asked.

"No," Sam said, looking worried. He looked again at his watch—2:45, about ten minutes since Pete's phone call. "I *told* you he's been kidnapped!"

"He has not been kidnapped," huffed Willy.

"Thanks for waiting, Sam," said Chris, getting worried himself.

"Guys," Sam announced, "I am *ultra-* worried. It's been fifteen minutes, and he *still* hasn't showed. The guard did not—repeat, did *not*—take Pete to the phones. She took him to the Administrative Offices area, which is where Scorpion Bluebird himself hangs out and is probably tying him to a chair right now getting ready to torture his eyeballs out!"

Willy rolled his eyes, "Oh, brother."

"I thought you liked the guy," Jim said to Sam.

"That was before this. Guys, you know how Pete is.

How he notices subtle things. Remember what he said? 'I don't trust the guy.'

"Think about it," he continued. "How did the guard know where to find Pete? How did she know what he looked like? Why did the guard take Pete to the offices—*that* way—instead of to the phones—*that* way?"

They stood there blinking at each other. There are only a few times when a clown like Sam will get serious. One of them is when he's totally convinced something is mega-wrong.

"And how come," Chris wondered out loud, "it was so soon after we ran into Scorpo?"

"Well," cautioned Jim, "we shouldn't jump to conclusions until after we've thought it through."

Ten minutes later, the others were as panicked as Sam. Whether he was right about the torture or not, it had been far too long for a normal phone call at a place where there were no phones.

"OK, my watch says 3:01. It's been thirty-five minutes, guys." Actually, about twenty-five. "What are we gonna do?"

"We should talk to Zeke before we do anything," suggested Jim.

"That's two hours away!" said Sam. "We gotta do something *now!*"

"No, I mean page him. We should at least find out what he says."

Sam's body language said, "Ack!" He was too wound up to be interested in trying to convince an older brother they weren't crying wolf.

Chris agreed.
Willy wasn't so sure.

If they look for Pete, turn to page 36.

If they talk to Zeke first, turn to page 21.

100

Sam broke off from the pack while the rest continued their romp around the second floor. It was weird for him to do that, they thought to themselves. But Sam had reached his limit. The sooner they left, the better.

Which they soon did. By 5:25, Washington, D.C., was sweating upon them once again. They sat their tired and hungry bodies out by the hot dog vendor to eat before heading home.

"Thanks for the tour, Sam," said Willy through a bite of hot dog.

"Yeah, we really saw a lot of stuff," said Pete, sipping on a soda.

"Told you you'd love it," said Willy to Pete.

"That 'Powers of Ten' movie was awesome!" said Jim. They all nodded.

Sam lay down on the waist-high wall where they were sitting. "Oh man, I could take a nap right here."

"Doesn't surprise me, the way you wasted yourself showing us everything," said Chris. "Sorry you were so bored. Guess we should make it up to you somehow, huh?"

"Be quiet, Kimosabe," said Sam, "or I'll take you through the Hirshorn. That place will warp your mind."

"What's the Hirshorn?" asked Jim.

"Thank you," said Chris.

"The modern art museum," answered Sam.

"Oh," said Willy, "you mean where they have paintings that are just like solid red and nothing else, or twisted pieces of metal?"

"You got it."

"Cool," said Willy.

"Sounds like you got your sense of humor back," said Pete to Sam. "I was beginning to wonder."

"Guess I take my work too seriously," joked Sam.

They laughed at that possibility, finished their hot dogs and sodas, and headed for the subway station. "Too bad Jill and Tina were at camp," said Willy.

"Yeah, they missed it," said Pete.

"Well, why can't we come back later?" asked Jim. The others couldn't see why not, and they sort of agreed they would have to do that sometime.

Sam sighed as they walked. The matter of secret tunnels had never come up. He had dodged the windshield of death.

At least for now.

THE END

Turn back and make different choices along the way, or turn to page 151.

"**W**hy don't you guys go ahead," said Jim. "I'll go wait at the Gemini capsule. If Pete really isn't kidnapped, he'll be there and I can meet him."

"And if we don't return by 5:15, you can call the FBI," added Sam.

Jim agreed to that, and they parted.

Chris, Willy, and Sam got into the offices by going through the staff lounge in the cafeteria. Sam led the way down several hallways and around half a dozen turns. He walked up to an unmarked door and opened it without skipping a beat. The others followed. They found themselves in an electrical closet.

"This is Scorpion's office?" asked Willy.

Sam faced the others. "Before we kick any doors in, I have a question. What are we going to do if we find what we're looking for?"

They hadn't thought of that. Sam and Willy looked at Chris, since he was sort of leading this SWAT team.

"I mean," Sam continued, "we can't just knock and say, 'Hi, we're here to rescue Pete. Please hand him over.'"

Willy scratched his head. "Maybe we *should* have called the FBI."

Sam and Willy suddenly realized how foolish they were being. If Pete had been kidnapped, there was nothing they would be able to do about it. Yet here they

were, huddling in a closet without permission, getting
ready to storm Scorp's office and declare a citizen's arrest.

"Yes, we can!" Chris answered Sam. "What's he gonna
do—shoot us? He'll have witnesses to deal with. Between
us three and Pete, he can't hold all of us. I'm telling you, all
we gotta do is find Pete."

Chris opened the door and stepped out, with Willy
and Sam close on his heels. Scorp's door was across the
hall, down about twenty feet. They could see the sign on
the open door, Martin U. Bluewater—Donations and
Acquisitions.

From where they were standing, they could hear
voices inside.

Downstairs, Jim had changed his mind on his way to
the Gemini capsule. He went instead to the phones. He
called his granddad and explained the whole situation.
Then he called Mrs. Andersen.

Pete was in an office down the hall from Scorpion's.
As he listened to his dad's half of the phone conversation,
he could tell his mom was on the other end. Kyle rubbed
his face and both smiled and grimaced. "Well Pete, I don't
think the guys got your message. They're coming to rescue
you."

"*Rescue* me?"

"Yeah. Jim just called Mom. Said the gang saw you
disappear with a guard and figured you'd been kidnapped
by Martin."

"What? Oh no!" he laughed. "What are we going to
do?"

"Well, I can't have them sneaking around, that's for

sure. All we need is for them to ruin six months' work. I just hope it isn't too late." Pete's dad alerted Security, then mumbled below his breath, "If this ever gets to the station, I will never live this down."

The "SWAT" team snuck down the hall, peered into Scorpion's office, and saw three people. One they didn't recognize stood right near the doorway; he was holding a laptop computer under his arm and was dressed like it was Saturday. Beyond him, the guys could see the woman who'd helped them at the theater. And standing behind a cluttered desk, holding a phone to his ear, was Scorpion himself. There was no sign of Pete.

"We're here for Pete," Chris blurted out as he stepped into the doorway.

"Pete?" asked Mr. Saturday.

"Yeah, Pete. We know all about your satellite encryptors. So hand him over."

"You what?" said the man in shock, looking Chris straight in the eyes.

"I said . . . ," Chris began. Scorpion's eyes went wild, and the woman in glasses looked back and forth several times from kids to Scorp to Mr. Saturday, with her mouth hanging open. Before Chris could finish his sentence, Mr. Saturday barreled right over him as if he weren't even there.

Chris lost his footing and immediately began falling backward. "The laptop!" yelled Scorpion. The woman started for the doorway. Sam was right behind Chris and started to fall, like domino number two, and instinctively grabbed the laptop to catch himself. Willy jumped on the guy's back and hung on for dear life. Mr. Saturday yanked the laptop from Sam and took off with Willy on his back. Willy started screaming.

Scorpion stood over Sam and Chris and ordered them not to move. They didn't.

It wasn't long before half the museum administration had filled the hallway. The offices emptied as curious and concerned folks came to see what the screaming was all about. Several guards appeared, along with several men in business suits—including Pete's dad.

It took some time before things returned to normal. Willy had made it back only a minute or so after disappearing around the corner, explaining that Mr. Saturday was in handcuffs. Scorp and the guards had herded Chris and Sam into Scorp's office and told them to stay there. Soon they included Willy in the bunch. Pete's dad locked the door

It was some time before he let them out.

THE END

Turn back and make different choices along the way, or turn to page 151.

"**O**h, that's all we need—," said Chris, "walk into an electrical closet with a hit man." These were wise words.

Jim got queasy at the thought. "Well, we shouldn't go in there anyway," he added. They needed all the reasons they could get.

"Why not?" asked Willy.

"Because it says Authorized Personnel Only."

The others blushed. Yeah, it said that, but they hadn't really thought of that as a problem. They had sort of gotten used to ignoring signs like Keep Out, Keep Off the Grass, and Authorized Personnel Only. It was good to be reminded that being Christians meant respecting property and obeying posted signs.

"What if we got in trouble?" Jim added. Maybe that would convince them.

"All for one and one for all?" Sam offered lamely. This broke the tension, causing a little bit of laughter.

"Jim's right," Pete said. "It wouldn't be right. Besides, it's not worth it, and I'm dying of thirst."

They all agreed and headed to the cafeteria for some pop.

CHOICE

Turn to page 46.

Pete panicked and took off running toward Skylab.

Scorpion looked shocked. "Oh!" he said.

They stood there looking at each other in a crisis of leadership. Back and forth they looked at each other, waiting for someone to do something or to give some sign of knowing what to do. After four *extra long* seconds, Sam took off after Pete, and the herd instinct did the rest.

"Wait!" Scorpion called after them, "I just wanted to apologize!"

They never heard him. "He went into Skylab!" yelled Sam, leading the pack. They had waited just long enough before following Pete that he was now out of sight. Walking as fast as they could through the crowd across the open courtyard toward Space Hall—the exhibit area where Skylab, the space shuttle, rockets, and the American-Soviet joint mission Apollo-Soyuz were displayed—they tried to catch glimpses of him but couldn't. It had gotten much more crowded since they first arrived. Or maybe that's just the way it seems when you're in a hurry and the crowd is in your way.

Skylab was a full-sized replica of the workshop part. It looked like a giant pop can with doors going in and out in the middle where stairs led to and from. It was one of those exhibits that people move through single file, slowly. Jim got ahead and started up the stairs.

"Wait," said Sam, "we can catch him coming out."

"Good thinking," said Chris. They went over to the other side and waited eagerly for Pete to reappear. When Pete still hadn't emerged after several minutes, Willy began to get restless. "What's taking him so long?"

"Maybe he's hiding," said Jim. He went back up the stairs to test his theory.

Jim exited alone. Pete was nowhere to be seen.

"I must have seen somebody else," said Sam.

"Where could he have gone?" asked Chris.

"Maybe he's back at the satellite exhibit," said Jim.

"Or somewhere else in Space Hall," said Sam. They decided to split up and try both possibilities. Chris and Jim retraced their steps through the satellite exhibit, while Willy and Sam combed Space Hall. They met back at Skylab, but without Pete.

Everybody was very frustrated and worried.

"OK, let's think," said Jim. "What did we decide to do if someone got separated from the group?"

CHOICE

If they decide to meet at the Gemini capsule, turn to page 32.

If they decide to report the missing person as lost, turn to page 121.

*N*ow?" asked Chris, though Pete was already lost in the crowd.

"Well, you know how Pete is," said Sam. "Waits till the last minute to do everything."

Jim decided Pete had asked the man if there were any rest rooms in the theater. He and the guys went in and saved a seat for him.

Meanwhile, Pete followed the man from a safe distance, his thoughts going wild. Why had the guy startled? Why had he said "Kyle Andersen," then got mad and denied it? Why had he walked away so fast?

For someone whose dad was an FBI agent, the answer was obvious. The kinds of people who would know Pete's dad and not like him did not come from church.

His dad could be in danger. For that matter, Pete could be in danger.

Pete got very scared and started to pray. *The Lord is my rock,* came the words from 2 Samuel 22. This guy could be a criminal out to get his dad. *My fortress and my deliverer.* This guy could be looking for his dad. *My God, in whom I take refuge.* This guy could be a hit man.

Pete stopped in his tracks. "What am I doing?" he mumbled to himself. "I'm following a hit man!" For the first time in his life—or at least since his cousin Wally locked him in the monster-infested basement when he was five—he began to shake uncontrollably with fear.

He made his way to a pay phone and called his dad's office with shaking hands.

"Dad!" said Pete in surprise, "usually I get Ms. Williford. I'm so glad you're safe!"

Mr. Andersen chuckled. "What's wrong, Son?" He could hear the trembling in Pete's voice.

Pete told his dad about the exchange in front of the theater.

"Well, I can certainly understand why you drew the conclusions you did," Mr. Andersen began, "but there's absolutely nothing to worry about. The man you met is helping me on a case that just happens to involve the Air and Space Museum."

Pete laughed a nervous laugh. "He really scared me, Dad."

Mr. Andersen laughed back. "Sounds like you scared him too. He was lying about knowing me. I'll have to ask him about that."

"There isn't any chance he could, you know, double-cross you?"

"No, nothing like that. He was probably taken off guard when he saw you and just panicked. We do look a lot alike, you know."

"Yeah, that's true."

"Just enjoy the rest of your visit and forget about the guy you met. Or better yet, go visit him. He works in Administration. Name's Mr. Bluewater. Tell him your dad sent you."

Pete laughed. "OK, maybe we'll do that. Thanks, Dad." Pete was near tears when he hung up. Being happy after being very worried can make you do that.

After the movie, Pete intercepted the gang at the exit and told all, but they decided to put off a visit to the offices until later. They hadn't seen any of the exhibits yet; they had to see something.

But the time went fast. Before they knew it, it was five o'clock and by then Mr. Bluewater was a distant memory. Zeke and the gang went home.

THE END

If you'd like to see what kind of adventures they could have had, turn back and make different choices along the way. Or turn to page 151.

Sam decided to try to get everyone to forget about the secret passages. Whenever the subject would come up, he would just downplay it or try to talk about something else. He hoped they'd just forget about it. If that didn't work, he'd try to unload the bad news and still come off looking cool, like he was just kidding. Either way, the idea was to avoid a messy confession.

His plan went into effect almost as soon as they got off the subway. He pointed out the plain, large, boxy museum made of alternating sections of solid white block and tinted glass. It looked, some of the boys thought, like a boxy caterpillar.

"Air-conditioning!" They groaned with relief as they passed through the revolving doors.

Once inside they could see rafters made of metal tubes attached to each other in triangles running along the ceiling. It looked like the drawings of space stations in science magazines. Hanging from these were airplanes and spacecraft of all kinds. The floor seemed almost littered with more of the same.

Before getting started, the gang and Zeke agreed to split up and meet back at the Gemini capsule at 5:15, fifteen minutes before closing.

Sam's main idea was to keep everybody distracted, and indeed the day passed quickly. Pete was fascinated by the satellite exhibit and read a lot of the signs, despite what he had said at the Freeze about "just looking at gizmos." Sam asked lots of questions, as Pete was a satellite buff. If it weren't for Willy, they never would have left.

Willy was happy as long as they kept moving, so Sam made sure they did. Except for the Flight and the Arts exhibit (which, he said, would be "*ultra*-boring"), he insisted they see everything, including all the movies. They almost succeeded.

Jim was easy to please. He was fascinated by everything, the high-tech stuff as well as the history, and even the strange customs of his American friends. They have high-tech stuff in Brazil, but the Air and Space Museum is one of a kind. And fourteen-year-old Americans just don't act the same as fourteen-year-old Brazilians.

And as long as no one brought up secret passages, Sam didn't worry about Chris. Chris enjoyed it because he was with his friends. He just wanted everyone to have a good time. He didn't have a dad like Pete and Willy and Sam, or a granddad as neat as Jim's, so he lived for times like this. The other guys didn't know this; still the fact that he kept his feelings to himself didn't make them any less real. So he made sure Willy and Pete didn't kill each other, translated "rewind it" and "knee slappers" for Jim, and laughed at Sam's jokes whenever humanly possible. Life was good.

For the most part, Sam's avoid-the-problem plan worked.

When he sensed they were running out of exhibit patience, he hyped the museum shop. This distracted them for almost an hour (despite what guys would like to believe about girls being the only ones interested in shopping). They talked about pooling their money and buying a model of the space shuttle, but in the end nobody bought anything.

They killed the last twenty minutes by plowing through the entire museum—every single exhibit—in single file. Sam led the way, pretending to be a tour guide explaining what passengers will see if they'll look to their right or to their left. They started at the north entrance, headed west toward the museum shop, and wove their way counterclockwise through every exhibit on the first floor until they were back at the entrance. There they switched around and headed for the escalator to repeat the process on the second floor.

They didn't quite make it before hearing an announcement that the museum was closing in fifteen minutes.

Sam breathed a sigh of relief. "Time to meet Zeke and go home!" he said.

"No," insisted Willy, "we've got to finish!"

CHOICE

If they leave now, turn to page 100.

If they finish plowing through the second floor before leaving, turn to page 66.

Jim gulped and gathered his courage for what he was about to say. "Guys," he said, "remember what *Ringer* means?"

"Yeah," said Willy. "'One who acts like someone else.'"

Jim nodded. "And in our case, the somebody else is Jesus. I just wonder if the Ringer thing to do is to sneak into offices and snoop around. If Pete really is in danger, shouldn't we tell somebody?" His heart was racing. He wasn't totally sure he wanted to be the party pooper, and he didn't know how Chris would react. But for some reason he said it.

They looked at each other in the tense silence that followed, both embarrassed and relieved. They felt guilty about sneaking around, but no one wanted to be the first to say it. Thanks to Jim, now it was out.

They talked. Chris explained that, to him, loyalty to Pete meant they needed to go find him as fast as possible. To Jim, it meant they should go to the authorities.

"I can see where both of you are coming from," said Willy.

Before long, a sense came over them all that the choice they would make was important. They were worried about Pete, and they wanted to do the right thing. It was this concern for a friend that gave them the courage to go to the cafeteria and pray.

They didn't pray long, just a few moments huddled in a semiquiet corner. But they all did it. They prayed that God would give them the sense to know what to do, that he would protect Pete, and that everything would work out. They wanted to pray about Scorp, but they weren't sure what to say. Chris just prayed, "Do whatever you need to do about him, Lord."

The amens were said, and Jim held up his hand. "All for one and one for all?"

"All for one and one for all!" they repeated to a mess of high fives.

"Ringers to the death!" said Willy, smiling.

"To the death?" winced Sam. "*Death?*" They poked each other as they got up to leave.

What they needed to do now was much clearer than before. They would look for Pete without being sneaky until the museum closed. Then, if they hadn't found him, they would call the FBI. In the meantime, there was always the possibility he hadn't been kidnapped at all. And, they had to admit, if they called the FBI now, they would say it hadn't been long enough for them to do anything about it anyway.

This was how Jim got his nickname: the Equalizer. Whenever the gang started to veer off from acting like Jesus' gang, he was usually the first to notice and to "equalize" them.

Sam led them into the offices through the staff lounge in the cafeteria. After several turns and intersections, they came to a hallway. Three doors down on the left was a door marked Martin U. Bluewater—Donations and Acquisitions.

"Martin, you Bluewater," Sam muttered. The others shushed him as they approached the door, quaking uncontrollably. They stopped before the door and took a deep breath.

Just as they were about to knock, the door opened. There stood Pete and a man they didn't recognize.

"Hi guys! What are you doing here?"

The shocked crew stood blinking and mumbling automatic hellos.

"Where . . . have . . . you . . . been?" Chris said, exactly like a parent about to unleash a year of harsh disciplinary measures.

"Didn't you get my message?" asked Pete, losing his smile. He could tell that they had been looking for him.

"What message?" Jim asked.

"The message about my dad asking me to stay here and how you guys could go home without me," Pete said. "He's here at the museum and . . ."

The man invited the gang in the office and closed the door. Pete explained everything. He and the other man were going out to get pizza when the gang showed up.

"You mean you weren't kidnapped?" asked Sam in a serious tone.

Pete just laughed.

"I am going to kill you," said Sam matter-of-factly.

Of course Pete survived Sam's attack, even if it did cost him a rip in the belt loop of his pants. But the guys couldn't stay; it was too risky. Besides, Willy knew his family was counting on him being home on time. So they were sent home, without Pete and without pizza. But they knew their friend was in good hands.

THE END

Turn back and make different choices along the way, or turn to page 151.

Pete was torn. He *really* wanted to see his dad in action. He'd never had the chance before. But then he thought of his friends—there they stood, waiting for him. They didn't know what he was deciding. He could make it sound like he *had* to go with his dad. But what an awful way to treat your friends. What would they think if he just abandoned them like that?

"I'd *really* love to, Dad, but . . . I guess it wouldn't be very fair to the other guys, would it?"

Pete's dad heard the struggle in Pete's voice, but he was not one to make decisions for his son, so he didn't answer. Secretly, he admired Pete for his loyalty to his friends and smiled to himself. "I'm sure the guys will appreciate your thinking of them. There'll be other times—I promise."

"OK," Pete replied, a little encouraged. They said good-bye and hung up.

"We thought you'd been kidnapped!" said Willy. Pete laughed. "Kidnapped?" He made it sound like no big deal, but inside he was also thinking, *Imagine that. Thank you, Lord, for such great friends.*

Chris was right. Just being together was an adventure.

120

THE END

Turn back and make different choices along the way, or turn to page 151.

They decided the best thing to do was to report Pete as lost. They made their way to the Lost and Found, which was at the security desk near the south entrance.

Chris stepped nervously to the front and cleared his throat. "We'd like to report a missing child." Not exactly what he wanted to say.

The girl behind the counter looked college age, maybe a little older than Chris's sister. She surveyed the gang and smiled. "How old?"

Chris blushed. "I-I mean, a friend of ours—he's lost."

"And how old is your friend?" she asked.

Chris could tell his answer was not going to have the right effect. "Fourteen," he mumbled.

"Oh!" the girl replied, nodding and smiling. "You want to leave a message?"

"Yeah."

She handed Chris a card and a pencil. "Make sure you print the name clearly. We'll hold it here in case someone by that name asks for it." She continued as Chris filled out the form. "You all should agree on a place to meet if you get separated. It's what a lot of people do because there's no way you'll ever find him in this place. Even on weekdays, you just never find anybody in a place like this. No way, too many nooks and crannys. Too many people."

"What should we say, guys?" Chris asked the others.

122

"How about, 'Meet us at the Gemini capsule'?" suggested Willy. Chris started to write it down. "Wait a minute," he said, "we *did* agree to meet at the Gemini capsule!"

"Thank you," said Jim.

Turn to page 32.

Jim yawned too.

"*Yes,* I see that tongue," said Sam, making Jim laugh. Soon everyone was either pretending to yawn or doing it for real, and they decided to take a nap.

The floor was hard and a little dusty, but pretty clean otherwise. There were a few pieces of brown packing tape lying around, one fluorescent light overhead, and one piece of brown shag carpeting underneath the two boxes, but other than that the room was empty. Not an ideal place for spending the night, to say the least.

Fortunately, there was enough room for everyone to lie down, but it would have been less cramped if the boxes weren't there. They thought about sleeping on the carpet, but the boxes were so heavy they couldn't get the carpet out from under them, and the room was too small to let them move them around very well. They soon realized they would have to lie down on the bare concrete.

"I wonder what Zeke is doing?" asked Jim as they tried to get comfortable.

"I don't want to think about it," replied Willy.

Sam turned off the light, and silence lasted for a few seconds. But before long a full-fledge gross-sounds-making contest was under way. Eventually, the gang had mercy on the genuinely tired Pete and decided to let him get some shuteye. Soon they all had given in to sleep.

"I don't know *where* they are," Zeke said into the phone. "We were supposed to meet at the Gemini capsule at 5:15."

Mrs. Washington, Willy's mom, sighed. "I suppose you'd better keep waiting. I can only assume they misunderstood where to meet you and went home by themselves—although I can't figure why they wouldn't have called by now. Well, at any rate, you'd better keep waiting there at the subway station. Call me back at seven o'clock or when they finally show. But you really can't leave as long as we don't know where they are. Sorry, Son."

Zeke growled in frustration and hung up.

Willy awoke with a start. Had he heard voices? He sat up and looked around. All the others were asleep. Wait a minute, how come he could see?

He turned around and found the source of light behind the boxes. He rubbed his sore spots and carefully crawled over Chris to the edge of the boxes. He looked down the narrow space between the boxes and the right side wall. He could see a little light coming from behind there, between the boxes and the back wall. And he could definitely hear voices, but they were way too muffled for him to make out what they were saying.

Willy leaned over Chris and whispered him awake.

Chris's bleary eyes opened just a little. "Huh? What?" The back of his head was aching from the hard floor.

"Look," Willy whispered, pointing to the back wall. "There are people behind that wall."

Jim awoke and sat up. "Willy," he whispered, "what is it?"

Willy turned around. "There's light coming through

the wall over here and people on the other side."

The whispering silence was broken suddenly by a loud "What?" Jim, Willy, and Chris shushed Sam frantically, Jim explaining quickly that there were people talking right next door. Pete slowly joined the blinking crew and picked up what was happening. As everyone rubbed sore spots, Willy repeated the news once more, and Sam turned the light on.

"So?" asked Pete, irritated at being awakened from a deep sleep.

"So maybe we can get out," whispered Willy.

"What time is it?" asked Jim, yawning.

Chris and Sam answered at the same time—"7:05."

"What are people doing in the museum at this hour?" asked Jim.

"Probably dying to go to the bathroom like I am," said Sam.

Pete lay back down. "Oh, I am so tired."

"We can get out! We can get out! We can get out!" whispered Willy excitedly.

"How do you know it's a way out?" asked Pete sleepily.

"It'd better be a way out or I'm going to have some serious trouble making it to nine o'clock," said Sam.

"Sam, why don't you crawl back there and check it out?" said Chris.

CHOICE

Turn to page 43.

Chris called his main rival, his older sister, Bonnie. She would sometimes give the guys rides, but she was a moving target—busy all the time. What some people call an overachiever. Chris hacked on her a lot, but secretly he wished he were like her. She was going into twelfth grade.

"Bon, can you give me and the guys a ride to the subway station? We want to go to the Air and Space Museum."

"Oh, I would," she said, "but I'm about to head out the door for a job interview. Sorry!"

"Rats," Chris replied.

"Enjoy the free time," she said with envy. "Some day you'll have to grow up and act responsibly, like me."

"Hopefully not," countered Chris, and hung up. Sometimes it seemed like the only way to do better than her was to try not to copy her. "Why do older sisters have to be so difficult?" he asked.

"Probably for the same reason older brothers do," replied Willy, thinking of his brother Clarence. "Except let's hope today he has a mutation of the brain and acts nice. Looks like he's our only hope."

CHOICE

Turn to page 39.

"**Y**ou know, Sam," said Betty, coming over to the table where they were sitting, "if you want to, you could help me around here today. I've got some stuff I'd like to clean out of the freezer, but I can't do it while customers are around. I'd be glad to pay you for it."

It was just the solution they needed. When they heard Betty's idea they all breathed a sigh of relief. This way they could go to the museum without torturing Sam, and Sam could stay behind without making them feel like they ruined his day by excluding him. Sam agreed to help Betty, and the others started to plan their trip.

"Just tell us how to get there from the Metro station, Sam, or we'll get lost," said Chris.

Sam drew a map for them. "It's really not hard," he said. "Get off at the Smithsonian Station, and you're within easy walking distance. Just look out for all the nuclear waste. It's everywhere."

They all looked at each other. "Nuclear waste?" said Chris.

"Yeah, when you get off the Metro station at the Smithsonian."

There was a moment of nervous silence. Then Sam cracked a big smile, and the others realized he had been kidding them.

128

"Nuclear waste, huh?" said Chris. "We ought to waste you!"

If they waste Sam, turn to page 34.

If they just go, turn to page 74.

Pete decided that joining his dad was just too good a chance to pass up. "I'll go with you, Dad."

"Great! The captain wants to meet you first—then it'll be official. Put the guard on the line, and I'll see you in a few minutes." Pete handed the phone over and explained to the guys. They were less than thrilled, but they didn't hassle him too much. They made him promise to tell them all about it when he got home. Chris felt, but didn't show, a twinge of jealousy. They parted.

As the guard led Pete through another glass doorway and the gang turned away, Pete's imagination filled with exciting scenes. *Surprise! Struggle for a gun. Pete diving across the floor. Chaos! Shouting! Gun shots. Flesh wound. Hero!* He smiled at the thought and was about to begin filling in the details in his mind.

"Must have been tough to leave your friends, huh?" the guard interrupted his thoughts.

"Yeah." Pete nodded. "How long will it take us to get there?" he asked.

"Not long."

They went down a long tiled hallway with doorways on either side every twenty or thirty feet leading to large open office areas. There were people working there. "Is this the office area?" asked Pete.

"Yep. But most of the real activity is on the other side,

behind us. That's where they process donations and acquisitions."

"You mean the exhibits when they first come in?"

"Yeah."

"Neat."

The place was abuzz with activity. Typing, phone calls, computers. It wasn't noisy or crowded, but there was definitely stuff going on. The people calmed Pete's nerves a little and gave him the courage to keep asking questions. "This is a strange place for an FBI sting," he said with a nervous chuckle.

The guard stopped him with a look of disapproval on her face. He had forgotten that stings are secret.

The hallway had several turns. They went through a kitchenette, two or three open office areas, and entered an unmarked door. The guard had to unlock it.

The guard and the three men in the room—Pete's dad, the captain, and Scorpion himself—greeted each other. "Hello, Pete," said Scorpion, smiling. Pete returned an embarrassed smile and a knowing glance. He wanted to apologize, but Scorpion beat him to it.

Pete's dad's captain had the look of a very serious man, with deep lines on his face that came from thinking hard a lot and smiling seldom. But rather than feeling sad for the man, he felt admiration. It was the look of a pitcher's face in the eighth inning when he's pitched a no-hitter so far and is trying to make it last. Dressed in a business suit and tall, he was even scarier, if that is the word, than Scorpion had been in front of the theater.

"I understand you want to join the FBI tonight?" He shook Pete's hand firmly without smiling.

Pete was sweating and his heart was racing, but he managed to stammer, "Uh, y-yes sir."

"Are you anything like your dad?"

Pete didn't understand the question, so he fumbled for something to say.

The captain said, "Loyal, disciplined, clever?"

Pete blushed and shifted nervously. "I-I try to be, sir."

He continued, "Pete, what we're going to be doing here tonight is called a closure. It's the culmination of a lot of hard work by a lot of people. It can all be ruined very easily. It's absolutely essential that you do exactly as any of us say at any time. Now we're pretty far from where most of the action will be, so it's likely nothing will happen here, but if anything does," he looked Pete straight in the eye, "you must do exactly as we say. Can you handle that?"

Pete straightened himself and said, "Yes sir!"

"It's also going to get pretty boring. A lot of FBI work is watching and waiting. Can you handle that too?"

Pete hadn't expected that, but he was determined. "Yes sir."

"Alright, you're in the FBI tonight, Pete," he said, slapping his shoulder. "Make your dad proud."

"I will, sir."

"Catch me a thief, Kyle."

"I will, Butch. Come on, Son, let me show you what we've got set up."

Scorpion excused himself with a wink at Pete. That

night, Pete had an adventure all his own. And so, of course, did the rest of the gang.

THE END

Turn back and make different choices along the way, or turn to page 151.

"**I** still think we should check the guy out, just in case," said Willy.

"Let's do it, then," said Chris.

They all agreed Pete shouldn't go first. That way if the man saw them, he wouldn't freak out again. Willy offered to go first, but then he always went first. Then Jim offered to do it. They decided to let Jim do it just to be different.

They walked up to the door, and Jim opened it. It was an electrical room alright, about the size of a bedroom but narrower, with cables and electrical panels running vertically along the walls. A ladder was chained to the wall on the right. Staring at them was a man in a tan uniform.

"What are you doing?" he asked angrily.

"Sorry," Jim said, and backed out as quickly as he could. Obviously the tall man hadn't gone in that door.

"Told youuuuuu," said Sam below his breath.

The uniformed man came out quickly and grabbed Jim by the arm. "If there's one thing we don't need, it's kids busting up the Air and Space Museum. Come on, you gremlins are coming with me." He led Jim roughly to a security guard out in the hall. The others followed. "These kids broke into the electrical room. Get 'em outta here."

They meekly followed the security guard to the security desk near the south entrance, directly across from where they had come in. Everybody was watching.

134

The guard told them to stay right there while he took down their home phone numbers. Then he proceeded to call each one of those numbers and to tell the parents that their kids were coming home. "Tried to break into private museum areas," he explained harshly. This was so embarrassing.

After paging Zeke, the Ringers left in shame. In fact, it was worse explaining to him than to their parents (you know how older brothers can be). Fortunately, nobody got grounded, so summer vacation was not totally lost.

Still, it would have been a lot more fun if they had found out what they did the easy way. Later that night, Pete kept his promise and learned as much as he could about the mysterious man. He told them all about it the next day.

"Wait till Jill and Tina hear about this!" they all agreed.

THE END

Turn back and make different choices along the way, or turn to page 151.

Pete sighed and combed his hand through his hair. He had been so excited and nervous he'd forgotten he needed to go to the bathroom. "I need to hit the rest room first, guys."

"OK," they all chorused, to which Willy added, "Do you want to meet us at Skylab, or do you want us to wait?"

"Wait up," Pete said. "All for one and one for all, remember?"

"Yeah," Jim said, "we can hit the water fountain. Your thirst will be my thirst, and your dryness of throat my dryness of throat."

They found the water fountain, but Pete's drink was cut short by a strange voice. "Pete Andersen?" it said. He looked up before he let go of the fountain handle and got his chin soaked.

It was a female security guard. "Y-yeah?" he choked, wiping his face on his shirt sleeve.

"You've got a phone call. Would you please come with me?"

He managed to say "Sure" and told the guys he'd meet them at Skylab in a few minutes.

"Got a date so soon, Pete?" teased Chris, causing the gang to laugh and Pete to turn red. "Don't stay out too late, Son," he called as they walked away.

The guard ignored them and led Pete up the stairs to the second floor.

That's funny, thought Sam. *The phones aren't up there.*

"How did you find me?" asked Pete.

"I had a good description," she answered. Then she shrugged. "And I got lucky," she added, cracking a smile.

"It must be important for you to try to find me like that."

She smiled. "Yeah."

They walked straight into the Flight and the Arts exhibit.

Sam was still watching them from below. *That's where the offices are,* he thought.

"Is something wrong? What's it about?" Pete asked, realizing as soon as he said it that she probably wouldn't know.

"I got no idea. That's none of my business."

At the far eastern end of the Arts exhibit was a set of double glass doors marked National Air and Space Museum—Administrative Offices.

The guard led Pete into a small lobby where a receptionist sat behind a large circular desk.

They take calls at the security desk, not the . . . "Guys!" Sam stopped in his tracks. "That's not where the phones are. They're over at the security desk—in the other direction!"

CHOICE➤

If the gang follows Pete, turn to page 26.

If they wait a little longer before jumping to conclusions, turn to page 97.

Zeke was about to give Sam all the reasons why they *shouldn't* call when he stopped himself. He was there to serve the gang, and if calling would give them some peace of mind, then— "Why not?" he said. "We got nothing to lose."

They made their way to the phones and called. They explained who they were, who Pete was, where they were, and what had happened. The man on the other end of the line listened patiently and was very helpful. He said normally it would be too early for the FBI to do anything, but since Pete's dad was an agent he'd look into it. He put them on hold for a long time. Eventually he came back and told them he knew where Pete was but couldn't tell them. All he could tell them was that he was definitely OK, and there was nothing to worry about.

That left a big mystery to solve, for sure. Where was Pete? Why couldn't they be told where? What was going on? Hanging in suspense is no fun, but what could they do?

Zeke and company had to wait until much later that evening to hear the story. In the meantime, they saw a few more exhibits and had fun.

THE END

If you're wondering what happened to Pete, turn to page 26. Or turn back and make different choices along the way. Or turn to page 151.

Willy started to get mad. He glared at Sam. "What is it you don't like about it?"

"I told you! I'm sick of the place!" Sam snapped back. By this time he was getting a little mad too.

"Willy, let's just forget it," said Pete, trying to avoid a fight.

Sam let out a big blast of a sigh, got up and headed for the door, muttering something about maybe they should go without him. Willy shot back that maybe they would. As he passed the trash can, Sam slammed his empty malt cup through the "Thank You" door. Pete yelled at Willy, and Chris followed Sam.

Sam had already taken off running and was clear down the street by the time Chris reached the door. No one could see that he was crying. Chris figured it wasn't worth trying to catch him, so he walked back into the Freeze and just glared at Willy as he sat back down.

"Well, I hope you're happy," he scolded.

Willy knew he had pushed Sam too hard, but he didn't want to admit it. He squirmed in his chair. "Look, you guys wanted to go too! Don't act like it was just me." He was right.

Pete acted surprised and said angrily, "It was *too* just you! It was your idea, and you're the one who kept trying to make him go."

"I was not! It was Betty's idea, and you pushed him just as hard as I did."

"I did not!"

"Did too!"

"Oh, let's just forget about it," Chris muttered. "I've got stuff to do at home anyway." He got up and walked out, not even remembering to say good-bye to Betty. Pete and Willy glared at each other for a few tense minutes, then went their separate ways.

Today, at least, the Air and Space Museum would have to host adventures for some other gang.

THE END

Surely the Ringers won't let a little disagreement keep them from having an adventure together! Turn back and see what other choices have in store for them.

They pounded and screamed for several minutes until their ears were ringing. Then they waited.

It didn't take long before the gang, half relieved and half scared out of their pants, could hear keys on the other side of the door. The door opened wide, and a big, husky man in a uniform with a pistol at his side scowled at the Ringers.

"Alright, get outta there, come on," he hurried them along out of the closet. They waited outside it as he relocked it behind them and announced into a walkie-talkie that he'd found them. Then he escorted them to the entrance.

Outside the museum, they found Zeke pacing back and forth. "What did you turkeys do this time?"

"We got locked in," said Willy, "and it wasn't our fault," he added quickly, knowing what Zeke was thinking. "The stupid museum locked up before we could get out."

Sam slipped Willy a smile.

"Held you hostage, huh?" Zeke said skeptically.

"Yeah," said Pete. "We got locked in a closet from the outside. Had to pound on the door until a guard came."

"A closet?" said Zeke. "Oh, I get it—it chewed you up and spit you out," he said, laughing.

"Back off, Zekehead," said Sam.

"Ee-yuck, this batch is rotten!" Zeke continued, making a spitting sound.

Sam leaped onto Zeke's back. The others quickly piled on, and soon Zeke was on the hard pavement beneath all five. "Gag me! Spit it out! Ugh!" he said, laughing.

Eventually he bargained his way out by promising to hold a Bugles Bash for the Redskins' season opener. Chris made him promise. "And don't forget the Oreos for Jill and Tina."

"OK, OK," Zeke wheezed. "Bugles and Oreos." They let him go.

Later on the subway, Pete remembered a question he had meant to ask. "Hey Sam," he said, "what was in those boxes in the closet?"

The other shrugged. "I don't know. I thought that was a broom closet, but I didn't see any brooms, did you?"

"I guess we'll have to come back some other time and find out," said Chris. "What are you guys doing tomorrow?"

THE END

What happens tomorrow is, of course, another adventure. For other adventures today, turn back and make different choices. Or turn to page 151.

Pete began to shake. "My name's Pete Andersen and my friends and I got locked in the museum accidentally and we found this hole in the wall and climbed out and were wondering if you could help us get out of here?" As he talked he was able to steal glances at the room hosting their little discussion. He would describe it as an office. A desk with a computer on it, a copier, filing cabinets, and a poster of the space shuttle took up most of the space. As Pete was talking, Willy stood up behind him.

The man scowled. "Go back where you came from!" he insisted.

"We can't because the door's locked," Pete said, glancing back at Willy. He was still shaking.

"What do you mean the door's locked?" the man asked in disbelief, standing. Pete didn't have time to reply. "How many of you are there?" The man started walking over to Pete, who by now was about to faint.

"Uh . . . uh," he fumbled, trying to count, "five, sir."

"*Five!*" The man cursed several times and grabbed Pete by the arm, moving him out of the doorway. Willy smiled at the man and waved. The man pushed Willy aside like he was moving clothes in the closet looking for the other three. Willy shoved his claustrophobic self past the man and into the room, visibly sighing with relief. The man noticed Sam coming through the hole at his feet and stepped back.

"You've got lousy timing, you know that, you punks?" the man said with a frown.

Pete gulped but dared not move. He began to wonder if he would survive this.

"On the contrary, Victor" said a female voice from the right side of the room, "I'd say their timing was perfect." Everyone turned around. The "voice" was dressed in a guard's uniform, complete with gun, standing next to the Federal Express box. Three men in business suits had entered right behind her.

Pete's shaking got worse.

One of the men quickly took over Victor's place in front of the laptop. Before anyone could say "Smithsonian Connection," the other two were within arm's length of Pete and Victor.

Victor cursed again.

Pete felt numb and started losing his sense of hearing.

"I got him!" one of the men said as Pete keeled over. The other moved Victor away from the boys and showed him a badge. "Dr. Straska," the man said casually, producing a set of handcuffs, "you're under arrest for theft and conspiracy to export stolen federal property." He then read him his rights. Victor did not resist.

Chris and Jim had been standing crammed into the back of the closet, straining to see and hear past Willy and Sam, who were too dumbfounded to move. "Mr. Andersen!" Willy began. One of the three newcomers had been Pete's father.

"What's wrong with him, Willy?" he said sternly, lying Pete on the floor and cushioning his head with his suit coat.

"I don't know!" Willy replied, eyes bugging out.

"Hold up his legs," Mr. Andersen ordered. Willy and Sam got on either side and obeyed. Chris and Jim emerged from the closet, blinking in amazement.

The men who arrested Victor escorted him out. Moments later, Pete came to. Pete's dad was the first to speak. "What are you doing here, Mister?"

"Dad!" Pete said. "We got locked in the museum. It was an accident. Total truth. We found this hole and crawled through, right into this. Is this really happening?"

Mr. Andersen just stared at Pete, trying hard to decide if he was hearing the truth. He sighed and looked over at the guard with a worried expression. "What did we get, Alice?"

"No promises, Kyle," the guard replied with a hint of amazement in her voice. "I'll have to check this out, but it looks like we got it all. The encryptor," she said tapping the box, "the schematics—even the backup floppies. And who knows what's on the hard disk," she said nodding at the laptop. "If I'm right, this one's a slam dunk, Kyle." She smiled at the guys. "Perfect timing, gentlemen!"

Mr. Andersen paused. "Unbelievable." Then, "Do you need any help, Alice? Looks like I've got an unexpected problem."

"No problem. We'll take it from here. You take care of the refugees. But we want to hear about it tomorrow morning," she ordered jokingly.

The bedraggled, loose-tied FBI agent and father of

recently-fainted Pete Andersen looked down at the gang. "Let me guess—you guys need a ride home."

"Zeke!" whispered Willy, suddenly remembering his brother. A phone call to the Washingtons confirmed Mr. Andersen's suspicion that Zeke had already left. At this point they could either go home alone on the subway, or wait about forty-five minutes and go home with Pete's dad.

CHOICE

If they go home with Pete's dad, turn to page 56.

If they go home alone, turn to page 41.

148

Pete looked at the guys and said frantically, "Guys—I've gotta go!" and broke off following the man.

Willy had already gotten his ticket torn, and Sam was next.

Chris looked back in surprise. He assumed Pete was announcing a trip to the bathroom that couldn't wait.

Jim knew little more than Chris but wondered if it had something to do with the man who was walking away. It would be up to him to decide whether to follow Pete or just let him go.

CHOICE

If Jim decides to follow Pete, turn to page 52.

If he decides to let him go, turn to page 109.

"This reminds me of the jungle," said Jim.

They all gave him a strange look. "Is it Skylab, or the tourists?" asked Sam.

"Neither," laughed Jim. "Once when I was seven, we lived near the jungle in Brazil. I wanted to go into the jungle to play with my friends one afternoon right before dark. I knew my parents probably wouldn't let me because they'd told me never to go into the jungle after dark. I almost didn't ask, but I decided to anyway. Well, they didn't let me go, and that night there was a terrible rainstorm. I might not have made it home if I had gone."

"So you think we should call?" asked Willy.

"Well, what would our parents want us to do?" Jim asked.

The answer to that was obvious. Sam led them to the phones. Pete fed one a quarter and dialed. "My dad's secretary hates me. This could be interesting."

"FBI," said a curt female voice.

"Hi, this is Pete Andersen. Is my dad around?"

"He's out on an important case right now, Peter, and he really can't be reached," said Ms. Williford. "In fact, he'll be out the rest of the day." Pause. She was both too old and too young to appreciate fourteen-year-old boys.

Maybe if he said it was important—"Well, it's kind of important."

150

She sighed. "Well, if it's *really* important, Peter, I *could* page him."

"Well . . ."

"Why don't you call your mother, Peter? If it's that important, I'm sure she could help you."

"Yeah," he said, giving up. "Thanks." Then he added quickly, "Could you tell him I called?"

"I'll leave a message," she said politely.

"Thanks." He hung up. "Well, so much for calling."

"What did she say?" asked Willy.

"She said my dad's out on an important case and can't be reached. She told me to call my mom."

"Your *mom?*" said Sam with a contorted look on his face. "*She* wouldn't know what's going on."

"*I* know that," said Pete, "but *she* doesn't. She *always* tells me to call my mom."

"Ms. Williford, I scratch my fingernails upon your chalkboard," Sam mumbled. This is what Sam would always mumble whenever a teacher would give a huge assignment or spring a pop quiz. It seemed to fit the occasion.

Once they'd tried to call Pete's dad, there was nothing left to do but get on with seeing exhibits. They decided on Skylab first.

Turn to page 135.

The Ringers' trip to the Air and Space Museum turned out to be a lot different from what they expected! You might even be curious about what would happen if they made different choices. If so, don't be shy—turn back and see what other adventures awaited them!

Make sure you haven't missed any parts of the adventures in this collection, and look for others to follow. Get to know Chris, Willy, Jill, Tina, Jim, Sam, and Pete. You may even decide to become a Ringer too!

THE END